My Assassin

Middlemarch Shifters 4

Shelley Munro

My Assassin

Copyright © 2022 by Shelley Munro

Print ISBN: 978-1-99-106304-5
Digital ISBN: 978-0-473-34950-9

Editor: Mary Moran

Cover: Kim Killion, Killion Group, Inc.

Munro Press, New Zealand.

First Munro Press electronic publication April 2016

First Munro Press print publication November 2022

For Paul.
Thank you for your unstinting support and love.

Introduction

One wrong move and her secrets will destroy lives.

Feline shifter Leo Mitchell is the pretty brother who attracts women with ease, but he's turned picky. He suspects the mystery blonde hanging around Middlemarch is the one for him. If only he could grab the elusive female and seduce her. Oh yeah. He craves some hot, sinful lovin' with the lady in black leather.

Assassin Isabella Black has harbored a huge crush on hunky Leo for ages. Because the timing sucked she's watched him from afar, praying another woman won't snatch the hottie away before she's free to stake a claim.

Finally the pair meet. Isabella offers her naked body but Leo counteracts with a cup of tea. Seems Leo likes to call the shots when it comes to sex. A day later they're finally dancing horizontally. It's smokin' hot, steamy, delicious—everything she's ever wanted. Isabella is ecstatic until another assassin threatens to ruin her happiness. It's life or death now. One wrong move and her secrets will destroy the Mitchells along with everything that has become dear to her...including Leo.

Chapter 1

Mystery Woman

The bastard was out there.

Like a predator, Isabella Black suspected he stalked his prey, prepared to pounce at the first opportunity. The same instinct that had led her to come outside and scout the vicinity told her he skulked in the shadows, concealed, waiting with patience.

With tension swirling in her stomach, she scanned the hills and rocky outcrops, resisting the urge to stomp back and forth in a show of frustration. She loathed this situation. It pushed her temper from calm to uncertain, which wasn't good for someone in her line of work. Her breath escaped in an impatient hiss.

At least the target remained safe, stashed in a secure house on an isolated farm. Felix Mitchell guarded his new family with determination and love. *As it should be*. He was an honorable man and perfect for Tomasine.

Isabella swiveled to scan the main road dissecting the small township of Middlemarch. The breeze ruffled her shoulder-length blonde hair, and she brushed it off her face with an impatient hand. She reached for the case holding her high-powered rifle. Assembling the weapon by touch, she loaded it, then held the rifle in her hands. Eyes watchful, she scanned her surroundings.

No strangers.

Not a thing out of the ordinary.

Then a flash of light, to the right of a leaning pine, caught her attention.

"Move again. Let me get a glimpse of you."

With infinite resolve, she waited until she caught the outline of a figure picking his way across the hill, slinking from rock to tree.

"That's it," she crooned, fingers flexing around her rifle. She watched him in her telescopic sight, noted his familiar features. One of Mika's cronies. Even if she hadn't recognized him, the weapon he carried gave away his purpose.

The man meant business.

Kill or be killed.

She aimed until his face lined up in the crosshairs of her sight and squeezed the trigger, feeling not a trace of remorse.

He fell, remained still.

A quick check ensured no one had witnessed the hit. Not a soul stirred, which wasn't unusual around Middlemarch since it was a country town. Isabella crept closer, needing to confirm his death for peace of mind. She watched the body up on the hill, frowned at his motionless form. A few seconds later, she slid through shadows cast by a sulky sun, approaching with caution. When he still didn't stir, she nudged him with her foot, stooped to check his pulse.

Dead.

She eyed him, the blood around his head and couldn't be sorry. A sleaze. The man enjoyed making his victims suffer, especially the women. Didn't matter how old, they experienced his special brand of torture.

"What the hell am I going to do with you now?" It wasn't as if she could leave him. Another body. Questions would be raised, but forensics wouldn't tie her to him, not even the bullets since she'd used her last African-bought bullet to do the deed.

Isabella went through his pockets and after careful consideration left his identification. He had a record and was no loss, although the local police might connect his body to the last suspicious death in Middlemarch. With a final visual check, she scooped up his weapons and retreated.

With the ease of practice, she packed up her rifle, strode to her bike. After stashing her weapon bag on the back and fastening her black helmet beneath her chin, she straddled the machine and started it with a throaty roar. She coasted down the hill, thoughts turbulent and worrying.

Another mercenary eliminated, which left Mika wandering the countryside. Time to flush him from hiding. As far as she knew, he was the last assassin after Tomasine. Originally, there had been eight. Over the years Isabella had taken care of the rest, but Mika was more determined than most—skilled and experienced.

A scowl twisted her lips. There was always the possibility Joseph had hired another batch of mercenaries to track Tomasine and assassinate her. She had experience with despots. They never felt secure until every single enemy lay dead in their graves. Their propensity for paranoia kept them alive.

Her features twisted into a full-on snarl. This self-imposed guard duty might continue for years, and her chances of an ordinary life...

"Shit." An unaccustomed burn at the back of her eyes made her blink, and she gritted her teeth so hard it hurt. The sliver of pain centered her, brought focus. A professional, she'd keep going until the job ended in a satisfactory manner.

No matter how long it took.

Isabella rode out of town toward Dunedin and the cottage she'd rented as a base, a place where she could relax and be herself. Far enough out of Middlemarch to avoid investigation by the Mitchells, their friends and neighbors, yet close enough for her to keep an eye on events as they unfolded.

Half an hour later, she pulled into a long driveway and sped along the tree-lined track leading to her rented cottage. Out of sight of the main road, she came to a halt and switched off the ignition. The silence always amazed her. Apart from the tweet of birds and the contented bleats from the flock of sheep in the neighboring paddock, a sense of isolation persisted. Weird how she now loved the countryside around Middlemarch. Even the frigid winter temperatures didn't faze her these days. The town had become home, drilling into her heart—

Isabella broke off the thought and chuckled—rich amusement of the type to attract masculine attention. "Double damn," she muttered as her traitorous body shot to full alert and the image of a man crept into her mind. Thinking about males wasn't the ideal way to go into a hunt. Thinking about a *particular* male rated as suicide.

With determination, she shoved the dark-haired Leo with the sexy green eyes from her mind and concentrated on business. She had to get to Mika and strike first. Lie and cheat if that was what it took. A derisive snort emerged from deep in her throat. More fabrications. She'd told enough lies to fuel winter fires in Middlemarch. Yep, they'd refuse her entry to heaven, but she'd do it again in a heartbeat if it meant winning this private war.

Isabella let her thoughts drift to another time in the past. She'd taken on the assignment several years ago. It had started as another job until a selfless act had her examining the path she traveled. In a flash, the scales had turned, weighing in on the side of right instead of loyalty to the person who'd paid her a healthy chunk of change for her services.

She'd shifted allegiance. No regrets.

Her conscience remained clear even though Joseph Magumbo made a powerful enemy. Since the change of sides she'd maintained silence, hoping those in charge wrote her off as a victim of her occupation. They might suspect nothing, or they could have a team of mercenaries tracking her, intending to strike her dead.

Yeah, wouldn't that beat all?

The assassin turning into the hunted.

Wry amusement broke in a single bark of laughter as she grabbed her weapon case and sauntered to the rear of the cottage. She tugged a single key bearing a yellow plastic tag from the pocket of her leather jacket. After checking the fine hair she'd placed across the door remained in position, she unlocked her cottage. Despite being alone, she pushed the wooden door open and slithered inside, casting out her senses.

Yeah, she hovered near obsession regarding security, but vigilance had kept her alive when others died. She did not intend to die at this stage, not when she had so much to live for. Hell, she'd even made a few friends—special ones—and wanted to keep them, which sent her back to Mika and his ability to screw with her future.

Time for a showdown.

Isabella relocked the rear entrance, walked through the spotless kitchen and along a narrow passage, passing a lounge sparse of furnishing before entering one of the two bedrooms. Her boots clattered on the polished wooden floors. A single bed filled most of the tiny room. Covered with a plain navy-blue duvet, it wasn't fancy or feminine, but the house suited her needs. She opened the door to the wardrobe, shoved aside leather jackets, jeans and a skirt to retrieve a black leather briefcase and put away her weapon case.

She sat on the edge of the bed and pulled out a satellite phone. Time to bait the trap to draw out Mika. Queenstown—a place full of tourists. Yes, let him get comfortable in the winter playground. She'd contact him, inform him she had a lead but required help. She'd entice him and knife him in the back before he knew what struck him.

Mika didn't stand a chance.

Restless pacing took Leo Mitchell from one side of the kitchen to the other. He passed the fridge, skirted the table with its fancy cream cover and vase of red and white flowers, turning before he collided with the new wooden bookshelf his oldest brother had built for Emily's collection of recipe books. His body thrummed with tension while his mind chewed over his problem.

His mate was out there. He sensed it with every particle even as he cursed his inability to find the elusive mystery woman.

According to Saber, mates converged together in a magnetic force of lust and attraction. His female acted plain contrary, intent on remaining hidden.

Hell, once he cornered her, he'd kiss her until both of them craved air then wring her stubborn neck. He scowled. Or he'd reverse the order. It depended on how frustrated and desperate he became meantime. This tail-chasing had become exhausting.

On his return journey across the kitchen, his sister-in-law Emily grasped his arm and yanked. "Stop! You're wearing a hole in my kitchen floor. Why don't you help Saber?"

"What?" Leo frowned at her, jerked from his thoughts of the mystery blonde who haunted him—the woman who might or might not be a danger to his family.

"Go. Help organize the hit on the madman in Africa," Emily ordered.

His lips quirked in unwilling amusement. "I never knew you were so bloodthirsty."

"Tomasine and Felix believe he's dangerous. We have proof of the atrocities the man has committed since Saber has double-checked everything before sanctioning the hit. I don't approve of people taking the law into their own hands, but he's a danger to us and the shifter species. He must be removed."

While Leo agreed with Emily, her ferocity diverted him. Both of his older brothers Saber and Felix had chosen strong mates—women he proudly called family.

Now, if only he could catch his mate. His muscles tensed, the inner frustration of knowing she was out there bringing a silent curse. He'd suffered through an icy shower this morning. A second didn't appeal despite the blaze of sunshine pouring through the kitchen window.

"Yeah. Okay. I'll see if I can help." To think he, along with his three brothers, had teased Saber, and according to his oldest brother, caused him premature gray hairs with their shenanigans. Saber had wanted them mated and had found his mate instead—Emily. Felix mated not long afterward with Tomasine, and damn if Leo didn't think he'd be next.

"Before you leave, Felix and Tomasine have asked if Gina can stay with us and go to school from here instead of learning by correspondence. I said I'd check with you first."

"Just Gina?" Leo asked, alarm surfacing. It was possible there were assassins out there intent on killing Tomasine, her daughter and foster child. Felix and Tomasine were working and living on a secluded high-country station a few hours from Middlemarch as a security precaution until they gauged the danger and squared it away. "Is something wrong?"

"No. They haven't seen a single stranger. There are no lurking assassins."

"That they know of," he shot back.

"Felix and Tomasine have decided on a regular high school for Gina, one where she'll find friends her own age. They're hoping to return to Middlemarch in six months. Learning by correspondence doesn't matter so much for Sylvie, but Gina is sitting exams this year."

Leo shrugged, thinking of the plump teenager and her determined efforts at flirtation. "Makes sense."

"So you don't mind if Gina comes to stay with us?"

Emily studied him until he felt as if he were under a bright spotlight. "Why are you asking me?"

"Because Gina has a crush on you, or she did. It's possible she's grown out of it by now."

Leo considered the teenager. Yeah, it was true she made him uncomfortable, but once she forgot to bat her eyelashes at him, it was different. Despite the age gap—his twenty-five to her sixteen—they had much in common. Leo liked his brother's foster daughter. "If it's okay with you and Saber, it's fine with me." It wasn't as if they'd spend much time together.

On a mission to find his mystery mate and corral her into accepting him, he might try Queenstown again since he'd sensed her there during his last visit.

"Good," Emily said. "Gina is excellent company."

"When's she arriving?"

"Today. She's grabbing a ride with an employee who is collecting supplies." Emily cast him a guilty look, and Leo stilled. Gina's return was a given even if he objected.

Too bad. He had more important things in his life than a teenager with a crush. He nodded and wandered off to find Saber. Not that he'd be much help in the illegal business. As the oldest in their family and part of the feline shifter council, Saber would have everything under control.

After an abrupt knock on the office door, Leo stepped inside. Saber had a phone clamped to his ear and his feet propped on the desk. The room hadn't changed for as long as Leo could remember. It had been Uncle Herbert's domain before the aged shifter had died, leaving Saber in charge. The desk was large, solid and made of native kauri wood. Shelves took up an entire wall. Labeled ring binders full of farm invoices and paperwork filled them along with back issues of farming magazines. On the far wall, Saber had hung several framed certificates, prizes earned at the agricultural show for their cattle.

"How much longer are you going to be?" Leo asked. "Do you want me to shift the steers?"

"The line is bad. Do you mind?"

"No problem," Leo said. "I'll take care of everything today. Take time with Emily. There won't be as much privacy once Gina arrives."

Saber grunted but didn't appear unhappy with the suggestion. Leo knew his older brother was pleased Felix had found a mate. The fact Tomasine had two daughters didn't hurt in a country community short of females.

Without warning, Saber took his feet off the desk. His alert manner told Leo he'd connected with the contact. Leo raised a hand in farewell and left the office, closing the door with a soft click.

He had farm work to complete and a teasing mate to hunt.

Late afternoon, after making the phone call and leaving a message to set up a meeting, Isabella rode into Middlemarch on her gleaming black Honda. She stifled the urge to hunt Leo Mitchell and instead headed to the garage on the outskirts of town where she kept her bike. Thinking of Leo and the decadent ways she could explore his muscular body drove her to distraction. It wasn't as if she could do anything to alleviate her simmering sexual desire.

The throb of the bike between her legs highlighted how long it had been. With a soft groan, she shoved both Leo and sex from her mind to concentrate on her surroundings.

Funny how the small country town felt so comfortable. Her home. She liked the way inhabitants helped each other in times of need. It had taken a while to become used to neighbors and family.

Family.

Isabella smiled. Another foreign concept she enjoyed. If things went as planned, one day she might have kin—her, a professional assassin. If anyone had suggested the idea five years ago, she'd have scoffed.

It showed how life had changed.

Isabella turned her motorcycle into a private side alley between two stone buildings before reaching the center of the small town. She slowed, switched off the ignition and kicked the bike stand before swinging her leg over the saddle. After unlocking the shed, she wheeled the machine inside.

A quick glance showed no one loitering in the alley. As usual, things remained quiet with school in session and most people busy with work.

A sigh whispered past her parted lips. Time to get this show on the road. She closed the door to prying eyes and pictured a dark-haired chubby girl in her mind. Shorter. Younger. And very different to her current appearance. With seamless precision, her body transformed, her black leather outfit melting away, merging with her skin. The surrounding air shimmered in a soft green—the same color as Leo Mitchell's gaze.

"Bloody hell," she snapped when the glow of light faded and her new shape had solidified. "Keep your mind on the job and off Leo." If she wasn't careful, she'd lose her edge, the thing that made her a good assassin.

Isabella took a deep breath and let out a hiss of displeasure when her breasts didn't so much as quiver. She scowled at the tight, pale blue T-shirt with *Sex Kitten* written in navy and silver on the front. She was coming to hate this disguise—a young sixteen-year-old. Where was the fun in that? Unfortunately, a necessary deception until she contained every threat against her adopted family. Then, she might attempt something resembling a normal life, start thinking of the future.

Isabella removed a bag of books from the rear of her bike and another soft bag containing clothes before leaving the safety of the alley. As always, she acted with caution, scanning the area first. An ingrained reaction, one that had saved her before. Leo Mitchell might offer a distraction, but she wasn't stupid enough to let him shroud her mind enough to forget basic security.

She meandered down the footpath to the Storm in a Teacup, Emily's café since Saber had purchased it for her. She nodded a respectful greeting at Sid Blackburn, a shifter elder, who exited the post office as she passed.

"Hello, lass," Sid said. "I didn't realize Felix had arrived back from his holiday. It's good to see you again. How is he doing? And your darling mother?"

Isabella chatted despite her urge to hustle. In the past, she might've led with a terse brush-off, but this polite conversation was part of belonging, part of being family. Even though impatience simmered, she kind of liked the friendliness of chitchat. "Felix and Tom are still up in Auckland with Sylvie," she said, sticking to the cover story they'd agreed for safety's sake. "I've come back early for school. Exams this year," she added, wrinkling her nose in typical teenage manner. "Tom didn't want me to miss my schooling."

"Aye, lass. Your parents have the right of it. Education is important in these times." Sid's forehead wrinkled with his thoughts. "Are you going to attend university in Dunedin once you finish high school? So many young people leave Middlemarch and never return."

"I'm not sure."

The elder sent her a hard, searching look before sighing. "You discuss it with Felix or Saber. They'll put you on the right track."

Or perhaps Leo. Isabella hoped he took a keen involvement in her future but confined her answer to a polite smile. She nodded and with a wave continued to the café. Anticipation lightened her step, and to her consternation, a hint of nerves lurched in her stomach. The unease scuttled like the ticklish steps of a praying mantis creeping around inside her tummy. A grin burst free—a natural one that hovered close to laugher. Her foster sister Sylvie's descriptive prose and vivid imagination had rubbed off on her.

On reaching the café, she took a deep breath, pushed the door open and setting the doorbell into motion as she stepped inside. She dropped her bags on the floor with a loud thump to announce her arrival and inhaled the spicy cinnamon of baking muffins.

"Gina! You're back." Emily ducked around the counter and enveloped her in a hug before pushing her away to arm's length to scrutinize her. "I believe you've lost weight."

It wasn't true, but Isabella grinned anyway. She liked Emily. In fact, she enjoyed all the Mitchell clan—those she'd met. They accepted her as part of the family since Tomasine had hooked up with Felix Mitchell. She'd always be grateful for the recognition because Tom wasn't her blood relation.

Unconditional acceptance wasn't something she knew. Fear, yes, but not love and friendship. She was a chameleon shifter, an assassin by trade.

Chameleons remained reclusive by nature, and on the rare occasions they mated, they produced a single offspring—if they bred with another chameleon. That was why she treasured the relationship she had with the Mitchells. They treated her as a member of the family, and a valuable one, although they might not return the sentiment if they learned the truth.

"It's great to be here. I've missed Middlemarch and my friends." Isabella glanced around the café, taking in the faces of the customers and classifying them for risk.

15

Visitors—tourists—intent on walking or riding the rail trail. *No danger lurking here*. She allowed herself to relax. "I'm looking forward to going back to school and seeing the gang."

Emily picked up a bag and drew Isabella behind the counter. "When does school start again?"

Isabella returned and grabbed her other bag before rejoining Emily. "Next week. I thought I might ring Suzie and the others and help you, if that's okay."

Emily patted her shoulder. "You don't need to. You help me enough during term time. Spend the time with your friends."

"If you're sure." Isabella had counted on Emily's good nature. Now all she needed to do was manage things so she could head to Queenstown for the weekend. If luck were with her, Leo would visit the tourist town too.

L eo wandered through the doors of the Queenstown casino, every sense alert for his mate. Even though he had no idea of her identity, he suspected it was the mystery blonde woman who had helped Sylvie—Felix and Tomasine's daughter—during her first unexpected change to feline. Sylvie had taken everyone unaware when she'd shifted for the first time at age five instead of the normal age of sixteen. It was lucky the unidentified blonde had been around to help the confused youngster.

After sifting through the jingle of the slots and loud chatter, plus the layered scents of perfume, cologne and pure excitement at the casino, Leo headed for the bar.

He'd arrived the previous evening and prowled the surrounds of Queenstown without luck, chafing at the denser population. He hadn't caught the faintest whiff of his mystery woman, and that made him yearn to shift to black leopard and run free across the hills to relieve his frustration.

It wasn't as if he could grab the nearest willing female and fuck the disappointment away, not when the female he desired was his mate. Damn woman. She'd mucked up his sex life but good. Leo snarled under his breath, cursing the fates and the heat prickling across his skin.

Without warning, Leo caught an elusive scent. A familiar one, it bore a hint of spiciness, reminding him of the wildflowers and grasses that bloomed around the salt lake in spring. He halted and almost caused a pileup of eager punters behind.

"Sorry," he said, stepping aside to allow the impatient patrons to pass and head for their gambling game of choice. He sniffed the air again. A mixture of strong perfumes and colognes. A whiff of body odor and musk and a hint of wildflowers.

It was his mate.

She was here.

Leo's heart squeezed out an exuberant pump, and he strode between the roulette tables, following the trail, his mood improving with his discovery. With no clear idea of her appearance, he scanned faces of women—both young and old.

Up ahead, he saw a slim form dressed in a black halter dress. The line of her naked back drew his attention, as did the gentle sway of her hips. Her fragrance.

His.

Leo quickened his pace until he stood right behind her. She had brown hair with reddish strands, not the blonde he'd seen or others had mentioned. A frown creased his brow. Maybe she wore wigs. Tonight her hair piled on top of her head in a complicated twist, the type that made a man hesitate and wonder if it were safe to touch. In the past, he'd made the wrong decision and suffered the consequences.

The woman ignored his presence, continuing her elegant and sexy sway while she progressed through the crowded room.

Damn. This mating business was tricky. More convoluted than he'd envisioned. *Show his face. Attraction. One becomes two—a couple.* Huh! Witnessing Saber's courtship of Emily and Felix's adventures with Tomasine should've alerted him to potential pitfalls. Like a fool, he'd relied on his natural charm and looks to ease him through without mishap. *Not working.*

The woman sashayed toward the bar, his original destination, so Leo followed while deciding how to approach her. Did he use a corny pick-up line, or did he bowl up to her and say, "You're my mate. Let's fuck and get acquainted?"

He snorted. Yeah, brashness would snag her interest all right—if she didn't run screaming for the cops first.

A man appeared in front of his woman. He spoke to her. Leo gaped in consternation when the tall male kissed her. And it wasn't a peck either. Tongue came into play.

Hell.

What did he do now?

His hands curled to fists, and he had to restrain his urge to choke the living daylights out of the male groping his woman.

She pulled away and laughed. Low and husky, the chortle twisted his gut and brought a wave of envy. Could a female mate with two different men? Leo sifted through the mating facts as relayed by Saber. There weren't that many and nothing he'd learned had prepared him for this dilemma. His younger twin brothers were both chasing Maggie, but they were a law unto themselves. They didn't report in often so their experiences were no help.

Leo forced himself to walk past to the bar. He slid onto a vacant barstool and ordered a dark beer. Meanwhile the couple entered the adjoining restaurant. A hostess directed them to a table in Leo's range of sight—if he craned his neck. They settled and accepted a wine list from the waitress. After handing over a twenty-dollar note and receiving his change, Leo shifted his barstool along the bar for a better view, sipped his drink and watched them with a mixture of irritation and pique.

The woman glanced up as if sensing his observation. Leo didn't look away but held her gaze, letting instinct guide him. Instead of glaring at him or glancing away, she returned his interest. A small smile played around her full lips. Her friend tapped her on the shoulder but she didn't return her attention to him straightaway. She winked at Leo before turning away to accept the menu.

Leo let out a breath, even more confused. He didn't know what to think or how to act. His logical mind anyhow. His unruly body had this bit memorized, and he shifted on the barstool to ease into a more comfortable position.

Leo continued to watch the couple. After consulting the wine list, they turned their attention to the menu. The woman scanned the dishes on offer and set her menu on the table. The male read it through, asked his companion questions and appeared to dither.

Score one point against him, Leo thought with disgruntlement. The stranger was good-looking with sandy-colored hair, or at least Leo had glimpsed other female diners checking him out and exchanging whispers. He was taller than the mystery woman and possessed hulking shoulders, although the suit jacket might hide a paunch.

Leo grunted. Mate or not?

Uncertainty made him reach for his drink. *Damn. Empty.* He signaled to the bartender and received another beer. After a third drink, Leo decided he was both sad and mistaken. This woman couldn't be his mate. He drained the last mouthful from his glass and stood. With a final glance, he turned and walked away.

Outside the casino, night had fallen despite the long summer evenings. A soft breeze ruffled his hair, bringing with it a whiff of exotic spices and Chinese food. Leo strode toward the lake, deciding if he couldn't shift and run, at least he could walk. When he passed restaurants lining the road, he heard flirtation, laughter, saw couples everywhere, their seats shoved close, heads together. Soft whispers.

Acute loneliness assailed him, joining the edgy anger and irritation bubbling inside. Poetic justice, according to his brothers, because women had fallen at his feet since he'd gone through the change as a teenager. His pretty face, everyone said.

Just as well he was here on his own, not with his brothers. Leo gave a wry grin before sobering. He could imagine the ribbing they'd give him. Nope. This was one of the times when solitary was good even if he reeled in confusion.

As he neared the edge of Lake Wakatipu, a tourist boat pulled up at the jetty. Passengers drifted off the boat in pairs. Leo's throat tightened, and he shifted his attention to the dark surface of the lake instead. Around the shore, lights twinkled while darkness shrouded the Remarkable mountain range that bordered the large expanse of water. Leo kept walking until the sounds of high spirits faded. Now and then, a vehicle passed, or he caught the drift of chatter and music from an open window. More couples. *Queenstown—a regular Noah's ark.*

Despondent, he continued to walk until he left the main center behind. Usually, the countryside soothed, relaxed him, but not tonight. He'd come out here to think, but nothing could get past the fact that the woman he wanted was with another man. Without being bigheaded, he knew he could woo and win another one, except his heart...his heart might break accepting second best.

Still out of sorts, Leo threw stones into the lake, the dull plop when the stone sank beneath the water echoing in his mind. He sat on the cool ground and studied the horizon with its myriad twinkling lights. After setting off from Middlemarch with such hopes, he'd plummeted to rock bottom.

"Hell, any minute I'm gonna break out with the country music." In disgust, Leo rose and began the walk back to central Queenstown and his hotel. He'd paid for the room so might as well use it. Instead of staying for the entire weekend, he'd check out tomorrow morning and return to Middlemarch. He needed advice, and he figured he'd find someone at home. Emily, since she specialized in sympathy instead of teasing.

Twenty minutes later, Leo walked into the foyer of his boutique hotel. It was exclusive and overlooked the water. He liked staying in the Wallace because the staff was friendly and efficient, the owner a fellow shifter, a widow whose husband had died in a car accident. Erin was older than him. Gorgeous and sexy, he wished she'd been the one instead of the mystery woman. They'd considered a fling, but with no spark between them, they'd left it at close friends.

"Hi, Leo," the night receptionist chirped.

He lifted a hand in greeting but kept walking. Instead of using the lifts, he climbed the stairs to his third-floor room. He plucked his keycard from his pocket and entered.

The faint scent of lemon polish and shifter combined with a foreign one—a hint of delicate flowers and a touch of spicy greenery. The maid had turned down his bed and placed a chocolate mint on his pillow. She'd forgotten to leave on the bedside lamp, which was a no-no in Erin's rules. The hotel proprietress liked to get the small details right.

Leo shut the door, pausing a moment to let his eyes adjust to the pitch-black. The faint rustle coming from the bed made him pause. He peered through the darkness, picked out the shape of a person and cursed under his breath. He didn't have the wrong room. The maid was going beyond the call of duty.

"Whoever you are, get out of my room. If you leave now, I won't report you to Erin." Leo sounded testy, but it had been that sort of day. He didn't have the energy to dredge up smooth, urbane and charming.

"I'll go if you want," a husky voice said. "But don't you want to see what you're rejecting first?"

The woman had the music of Europe in her speech. French or Italian. Something continental and familiar.

"Turn on the light." Leo held his breath, distrusting his senses.

The crisp cotton sheets rustled. Leo's heart raced. This was his mate, and she was waiting in his bed. His lungs expanded while he tried to exert control on his body. Not a single thought of cold showers or icky situations worked on his eager dick. It felt as if every drop of blood had sunk to his groin while he waited for illumination.

23

After a soft descriptive curse that raised a grin in Leo, she found the light. It flicked on, spotlighting the bed. Leo gaped. The female in his bed wasn't wearing anything except a come-hither smile.

It was her—the mystery woman.

Chapter 2

Queenstown Sojourn

L eo didn't move, not even to cover his painful erection. He stared at her, uncertain of where to start, what to say. Finally, he swallowed and cleared his throat. "What are you doing here?"

A delicate brow arched, and a smile formed on her luscious pink lips. She tossed her head, her brown hair brushing the tops of her shoulders now that it was loose instead of piled on top of her head. "Isn't it obvious?"

"No." His gaze drifted across the creamy skin of her shoulders and the shadowed curves of her breasts before raising his eyes to scan her face. She wore a soft smile that showed straight white teeth. Her bold features, softened by the smile and the gleam in eyes neither blue nor violet but a shade somewhere between, held amusement.

"No? Should I be even more forward?"

Her foreign accent—Italian, he decided—sizzled along his nerve endings in a seductive manner. Leo wanted to ask her questions so he could hear her musical tone yet again.

"I can do brazen with the best," she murmured, and with that, she swept aside the white cotton sheet covering her body.

Leo's breath caught. He couldn't have looked away if he tried. The woman was sleek muscles and curves with generous breasts. His fingers itched with the desire to touch. His befuddled mind took in the fact she was not a blonde. The color of the hair on her head was natural. Leo took one step closer to the king-size bed and halted. "Why are you here?"

She tipped her head to the side and regarded him with a patient smile—the kind a parent gives a child. "I'm disappointed with your intelligence, but your looks make up for the lack."

"There's nothing wrong with my IQ," Leo snapped. But it was true his brain had turned sluggish. A man had his pride when it came to a potential mate. He refused to settle for a one-night thing, and he sure as hell wasn't taking any man's leavings.

"Should I take charge of the seduction?"

Leo folded his arms across his chest and concentrated on her face. He didn't trust himself to look at her breasts for an instant longer. "I want answers," he said in a hard voice, "and if I don't get them soon, I'm calling security."

"I'd like to see you try," the woman retorted. "You'll look stupid, no matter what you tell them."

Erin's involvement would also suck. "Who are you? What's your name? What are you doing in my room?" Leo fired questions, desperately wanting answers before she wriggled past his control and he succumbed. He was a hairsbreadth from turning caveman and jumping her. Not a bad idea except damn if he intended to steal a woman off another man, or mate with a woman short on morals.

"My name is Isabella Black. I saw your interest in the casino." She lowered her voice to a seductive purr. "I liked what I saw and decided to extend an invitation."

"An invitation to what?"

"Time's ticking. This was a one-time-only offer." The woman stood and turned away to retrieve her clothes from a chair where she'd left them neatly folded. Although she covered it well, he sensed her disappointment.

"Wait!" Hell, nothing was running to expectation. He'd had visions of a romantic dinner, a getting-to-know-his-mate meal, letting the awareness between them simmer, the heat rising until it boiled into passion.

"Wait for what? A cup of tea?" She toyed with her clothes but didn't start dressing. Her arse was world class, and she had a sexy green dragon tattooed in the small of her back.

"I can make tea." Leo worked at keeping his voice even. He'd love to inspect the dragon at closer quarters, drag his tongue across the green body, nibble a bit. Taste.

27

"But I don't want tea," she whispered, turning to face him. "I want sex. Hot, sweaty, no-holds-barred sex." Her lips pursed and when she saw she'd caught his attention, her tongue darted out to moisten her lips. One sweep and they glistened.

Leo scowled. "You're a stranger."

The woman—Isabella—laughed, but the sound held not a shred of amusement. "You're a disappointment, Leo Mitchell. I'd heard you're a charming daredevil up for any challenge. Don't you want me?" She sashayed across the carpeted floor, stopping mere inches from him, close enough so he felt the heat coming off her body. "Can I tempt you?" Her breath puffed across his lips, tickling and seductive. He glimpsed her tongue poking between her lips and the vise around his chest tightened a notch.

He retreated a step. He couldn't think with her enticing body so close and her delicate scent teasing him, seducing him. Could she tempt him? *Hell, yeah*. But that didn't mean he was going ahead. A man had to have some scruples. Leo Mitchell didn't steal another man's woman.

"Who was the man?"

"A friend." She didn't pretend to misunderstand, and that scored points with him.

"Do you play tonsil hockey with all your friends?"

Isabella shrugged, hard enough he couldn't fail to notice the jiggle of her breasts. "Mika has a warped sense of humor. It was a joke. We were lovers, but now we're friends with good memories."

Leo wanted to believe her. *Toss his scruples. Okay for women to act the aggressor.*

Yet, somewhere along the line, his mind refuted the fact.

His alpha feline genes snapping to attention.

"What were you doing in Middlemarch? How did you know my name?"

"Where? I overheard the maids gossiping. That's how I learned your name." Her cool reply contained just the right amount of surprise, but Leo knew better. The woman held her secrets close. Understandable.

But he didn't make mistakes. He recognized her scent. It bloody haunted him.

"How did you get in here?" Okay, he'd ignore the Middlemarch thing for now. He'd caught a fleeting glimpse and thought she was Sylvie's mystery helper, even though the hair color was different. He'd ferret out the truth later. "Do you have a key or did you bribe a maid to let you inside?"

Isabella grinned and reached out to brush her hand over his cheek. He jerked away. Damn, he'd felt her touch clear to his toes. Leo retreated farther, uneasy with her taking charge of this meeting.

It was his room.

She was the intruder, not him.

Her grin widened, and it pissed him off. He glowered but her sassiness remained intact.

"Anyone would think I frightened you."

And they'd be right. She was his future. "I'm not frightened of you."

"Then why are you running?"

"You're a stranger." Leo shoved his hands in his pockets. "You're stark naked and you broke into my room." One distraction required, something to quash his desire to stroke her sleek muscles and explore her body with fingers and mouth.

He wanted to win her on his terms, dammit.

He wanted the thrill of the chase.

Chapter 3

Offer and No Acceptance

I sabella stared at Leo, trying to hide the fact the male nonplussed her. Yet again, he displayed the integrity common to every Mitchell of her acquaintance. Heck, she'd offered herself on a plate.

"I want you," she fired back after taking several rapid breaths. They did little to disperse her irritation or the embarrassment crawling through her veins. With his refusal, he'd made her small—a two-inch-high bimbo.

Rejected yet again.

Memories of Gregory, an ex, assailed her, but she pushed them away. Determined, Isabella took one more calming breath and forced her features into an amused smile. "I thought that was what you wanted."

"I prefer to do my own hunting." Leo's flat tone told her she'd messed up big time. But he'd wanted her in the casino. She'd sensed his attraction, so what did she need to do to prod him to action?

Why did the man's straight and honest streak have to show up now? Isabella wanted to screech her frustration but refrained since a fuss would attract security, and besides, assassins didn't resort to feminine hysterics, no matter what the stress factors. Ill-discipline led to an early death. No, assassins remained calm and cool under fire. She should look upon this as an unexpected curve ball in her latest assignment. A challenge.

"You should dress. We don't want you to catch cold."

Isabella's mouth dropped open. Before she could react further or throw herself into his arms, Leo strode into the bathroom and returned with a navy-blue robe. He held it up, ready for her to don, a silent demand.

Ooh, alpha male with excellent manners. A shot of heat suffused her body, gathering low and coalescing into a needy ache. It wasn't often a man treated her as a lady, and it was heady stuff. After meeting his steady gaze for an instant longer, Isabella accepted his determination. With a testy sigh to make her feelings known, she acquiesced to his wishes but accepted the robe with ill grace. She thrust her arms into the sleeves. Dammit, she'd been patient. Her serenity and willpower had scrubbed away, leaving simmering impulsiveness in its place. Frustrated hormones filled every inch of her body. *Just call her horny*.

There was nothing wrong in going after what she wanted. Nothing.

Too bad if Leo Mitchell was slow on the uptake. He was a doomed man in the sights of an assassin. He didn't stand a chance.

Isabella peeked at him from between lowered lashes, taking in his stubborn expression and tight jaw, the tense set of his broad shoulders. It didn't look as if he'd change his mind tonight, but then tenacious was her middle name. Some people might call her single-minded or worse, a hard-ass. Guilty on both counts.

Her breath eased out with longing while her gaze caressed him. Tummy-tingling and striking in his black dress trousers, cream linen shirt and black leather jacket. Tasty. She loved the way he smiled and his lazy good humor, laced with more than a hint of charming rake. With his dark hair, intense green eyes and strong nose, a jaw shaded with shadow, he looked good enough to eat. For so long she'd fantasized about the body beneath the clothes with the occasional glimpse to keep her hopes alive and hormones hopping. Time to unwrap the parcel, to take a step or two in a new direction. She tightened the belt of the robe around her waist.

"That's better," he said with relief.

Isabella's eyes narrowed on the slow-witted male, her self-confidence taking a momentary dive. Wait. This was her man. He just didn't know it yet. Yeah, she'd lull him with cooperation and jump him later, taking advantage of his low defenses.

"I'll take that tea now." *Hot tea. Huh!* A poor sexual substitute. Dammit, this wasn't fair. She glared at him. "Are the rumors I've heard exaggerated?"

Leo paused his search through the tea bags provided by the hotel. He glanced over his shoulder, keeping his gaze on her face and away from the creamy cleavage she'd carelessly displayed for his benefit. "What rumors?"

"I heard you were an excellent lover." Isabella suppressed a shudder of pure need, her nipples drawing tight against the nubby fabric of the robe. Leo knew how to satisfy a woman. The bad-boy twinkle in his eyes spelled it out for any woman to discern. The male was being plain mean, making her wait and suffer. She sat on the bed, ignored the irritated slitting of his eyes and regarded him with a façade of calmness. "Were they wrong? Do you need little blue pills?"

"Blue... I don't need to defend myself to you. But for the record, I prefer to do the asking. I'm old-fashioned that way."

"It's not wrong to strive for what I want." Isabella watched him for the slightest reaction. Difficulties ahead. Easy to see. A relationship with Leo would not be easy, not with the lies and half-truths between them. And his stubbornness was an added difficulty. Too bad. Time to make a move. She'd noticed his edginess, how restless he'd become and how often he'd traveled to Queenstown. She hated him being with other women. He was ready to mate, and lucky for him, she was his other half.

He just didn't know it yet.

A pity he'd chosen the same weekend as Mika. Isabella had seen Leo's expression when he'd noticed her with the assassin, the flash of temper and the possessive stamp on his features when the other man had touched her shoulder. In the past, Isabella might have scoffed at the mention of a fated mate—a bond between male and female so strong there could be no other. That was before she'd met the Mitchell family. Isabella chuckled at the thought. Who'd have thought? A mate...

"What's so funny?" Leo placed a steaming cup of black tea on the bedside unit. He plucked several sachets of sugar and two small plastic milk containers from on top of the minibar and set them alongside the tea.

"Nothing." She studied the familiar angles of his face and her heart pitter-pattered. Dark brows slashed above his eyes, and he hadn't had his hair cut for a while. It fell in natural curls. Thick lashes surrounded his green eyes while his lips were firm. Sensual. She couldn't wait to take a taste. For so long, she'd fantasized about making love with Leo, touching him intimately. She eyed her tea, trying to remember the last time a man had waited on her without expecting sex in return. Her heart went pitter-patter all over again.

"You remind me of someone," he said, making her aware he'd scrutinized her as intently while she'd cataloged his sexy features. She shifted her weight and thrust out her breasts, taking pleasure in the way he followed her subtle move.

"A lover?"

"No," he said with a hint of bite. "You shouldn't listen to rumors. Despite the maids' gossip, I don't bed every woman who crosses my path." His face darkened with indignation and a touch of impatience. "You still haven't told me how you entered my room. I should call hotel security."

"But you won't do that to little old me. Will you?" She wasn't stupid enough to confess regarding her special skills—not right now at any rate. She required more time to prepare the way. Acceptance of a lover who appeared permanently green and ugly in their natural state took bravery and trust. Green might work for an animated cartoon character, but in real life the color scared people. Yep, best she made sure he was enamored and loved her unconditionally before she spilled her secrets.

She glanced at him again, making sure her face remained impassive and displayed none of the yearning coursing through her veins. The inability to bear children to anyone but another chameleon might prove an obstacle too. Men like Leo wanted sons and daughters. She'd watched him with Sylvie and knew how cool he was when he interacted with Gina in her awkward, chubby, sixteen-year-old guise. Isabella swallowed a sudden attack of doubt. Was she wrong to take this step? Once taken, she couldn't retreat. Everything would change. She couldn't reverse her actions.

It was all or nothing.

She reached for the cup and sipped the steaming tea, ignoring both milk and sugar. Isabella Black didn't take milk or sugar while Gina did. Different characteristics for each persona. Part of being an excellent assassin—attention to detail and the ability to blend. "What would make you change your mind?"

"About taking you into my bed?"

Impatience bubbled free. "Your questioning mode is tedious."

Leo regarded her with a control rivaling her own. "Answer my questions and we can move on."

Yes, please. Dammit, she'd love to step into a new future. It was the reason for this confrontation. Time to change tactics. Despite the easygoing manner he portrayed, tonight had shown him as staunchly conservative. She'd made a mistake by trying seduction.

Leo Mitchell needed finessing.

"I timed my arrival with the room maid and spun her a story about meeting my fiancé here to surprise him." She read people to survive—another one of her assassin skills—but she wasn't doing such a sterling job tonight.

At home, interacting with the family, he always acted so carefree with the same underlying confidence and integrity all the Mitchell brothers exhibited.

A sigh escaped, and in that moment, she decided to risk everything. "I'm sorry I've made you uncomfortable." She reached over, intending to set her tea on the side cabinet. The neckline of the robe gaped, but she ignored it. "I'll leave."

Leo dropped onto the navy easy chair sitting near the curtained window and studied her in a pensive manner.

"Your tea is getting cold. You're the one who wanted it." His scrutiny brought agitation to the surface, but she couldn't look away. Need throbbed inside, the plain edginess simmering between them, sensitizing her body.

Humor lurked in his eyes, as if he knew how unsettled he'd made her, before fading to intense and curious. She tightened her grip on her cup and focused on the low-level heat emanating through the china as a means of distraction. The need to jump him flowed through her like a fast-acting drug, but she resisted. Isabella never made the same mistake twice.

Leo rose to pace the length of the hotel room, his footsteps muffled by the thick woolen carpet. She admired the familiar fluidness of his moves, his tight ass, and her desire ratcheted up a notch. Her mouth dried, and she swallowed, attempting to moisten it while willing herself to remain seated, keep her hands to herself.

Good things came to those who waited. She reminded herself of the fact even though the cliché lacked comfort. Leo prowled toward her and stopped in front of the bed where she sat.

"Come out with me tomorrow on a picnic." Leo's voice held confidence, dammit, and it aggravated her. He snapped his fingers and expected her to jump?

Isabella sipped her tea, concentrating hard on keeping her mouth shut. Now he thought she was easy. Part of her wanted to say no, but childishness would be counterproductive to her plan. She'd arranged to meet Mika early tomorrow morning because her fellow assassin intended to follow up a lead in Auckland. "What time?"

"Say around eleven. I'll arrange a packed lunch." He stopped by the phone and scooped up the small notepad and pen provided by the hotel. "What's your address? Where will I pick you up?"

Isabella suppressed a smile. He sure liked his questions. "Room 314, Wallace Hotel."

Leo gaped at her, his green eyes flashing surprise. "That's the room next to me."

"That's right," Isabella said, knowing he'd be wondering why he hadn't sensed her presence. Mentally, she snapped her fingers at him in a cheeky manner. Simple, for a chameleon.

"But—"

Isabella stood and gathered her clothes. "I'll return your robe in the morning." She sauntered to the door, the weight of his bemused stare on her back the entire way. Surely, Leo Mitchell hadn't thought he'd have everything his own way?

Leo woke after a few fitful hours' sleep. The bloody woman was staying right next door, and he hadn't had a clue. Whenever he saw her, his senses roared she was his mate, so why had he missed her presence?

And the hair color—why had she worn a wig? Leo grinned. He couldn't wait to discover but on his terms. Not hers. He snorted when he remembered her brazenness. Women had tried to get their hooks into him before but he'd evaded with no regrets. This time felt different. Just looking at her did things to his libido, pushing him into a cycle of lust and a yearning to mark her as his property.

Hell, hark at him.

A chattel.

Emily and Tomasine would geld him if he verbalized the thought. Isabella might help. Truth was, despite the mating heat, he refused to act the Neanderthal. There were better ways of taming a woman.

"Isabella." Leo tried her name for size, rolling the syllables as if they were a delectable mouthful of chocolate. "Hell, man. You've lost it," he muttered, but he grinned all the same.

After glancing at the radio clock on the bedside table, he reached for the phone and rang the kitchen to order a lunch basket for two. The chef made a few suggestions, and Leo hung up with a sense of satisfaction.

He relaxed against the white pillows in a casual sprawl. On their Uncle Herbert's recommendation, his older brother Saber had purchased land outside Queenstown. Grape vines covered part of the land with wine tasting and a restaurant on premises. Their award-winning Pinot Noir wines were both popular and profitable. He'd take Isabella Black, mystery woman, to picnic on their private land, a place free of interruptions.

Today, he'd gain the upper hand. Yeah, he'd find a special way to make her purr.

Leo pondered her and shook his head in amusement. Maybe not. The mystery woman had her own agenda. Impulsive. Unpredictable. The uncertainty involved brought anticipation and eagerness of the sort he hadn't experienced for ages.

Last night had thrown him. He hadn't liked her thrusting him into the role of pursued. A smirk formed on his mouth. No getting away from it—he was feline through and through and loved the chase, the stalking. The final victory of capture.

Compliance.

Today, Isabella Black would have her hands full. He'd make sure of it.

Knuckles rapped on his door. Leo leaped from bed and yanked on a pair of jeans before answering the summons.

It was Isabella. Her brown hair tumbled in a sexy curtain around her face and shoulders, a fringe framing her eyes. Bluer this morning than violet, they shimmered with silent laughter. "Good morning."

Leo wanted to kiss her but made do with a smile. She was trying to direct things again. While he wanted her to stop, part of him wanted to learn the lengths she'd go to in order to gain his attention. "Morning."

"Would you have breakfast with me in the restaurant?"

"I'll meet you there in half an hour." Leo shut the door in her face. His sharp hearing picked up the huff of annoyance and he smirked. He looked forward to an interesting day.

Exactly half an hour later, Leo walked down the stairs to the ground-floor restaurant. Erin was on duty, directing guests and diners to their tables.

He brushed a casual kiss over her cheek. "Morning, sweetheart."

"You don't normally have breakfast," Erin said in surprise.

"I have a date." Leo scanned the restaurant and saw Isabella sitting at a table overlooking the lake. "She's over there. Talk to you later." Ignoring Erin's raised eyebrows, Leo strode to the table where Isabella waited.

"Good morning again." God, she looked gorgeous with the sun hitting her hair and gilding the red strands with fire.

He gave in to temptation, leaning closer to cup her face in his hands and taste her mouth. He'd planned an easy exploration, just a quick sample, but his good intentions fled the instant she responded. The slow slide of her tongue into his mouth shot urgent hunger straight to his groin, and he went with it, deepening the kiss and yanking it into carnal territory. Their tongues flirted, explored. Sipped. She moaned and damn if he didn't want to moan his own pleasure aloud too.

"That's enough of that," a familiar voice said.

Shocked, Leo jerked away from Isabella and whirled to face Erin. "I—"

"Sit. Stop making a spectacle of yourself." Although her voice sounded stern, Erin had a twinkle in her eyes.

Flummoxed, he dropped onto the chair opposite Isabella. From zero to ready for action in seconds flat. *A first.* Through narrowed eyes, he studied Isabella, who looked as cool as an icy beer on a hot Otago day.

Erin's mouth kicked up in amusement. He'd face questions and teasing later once she cornered him in privacy. "You can order off the menu or partake in the buffet breakfast."

"Coffee and the full-cooked breakfast, thanks," Isabella said.

"I'll take the same please, Erin." Longer to spend with the mystery woman and learn what made her tick.

Erin nodded and accepted the menus back before heading off to deal with other hotel guests seeking breakfast.

"A lover?" Isabella asked, her brows drawing together in a frown.

"Not now." Leo snared her hand, the urge to touch a compulsion. Her hand for now. But later...later, he'd expand his exploration zone. Scheduled to *his* plan of course.

"Are we going to become lovers today?"

Leo's mouth dropped open, and he snapped it shut. Did she have any idea what her loaded questions did to him? The naughty twinkle in her eyes said *hell, yes*. The minx knew. "We'll take the day as it comes. That way neither of us will suffer disappointment."

"You want me."

Persistent. Any other woman behaving in this manner would send him fleeing in the opposite direction, but something about Isabella fascinated him, so he suffered her outrageous comments.

Leo turned her hand over and lifted it to his mouth. He kissed the delicate skin at her inner wrist and let his tongue dart out for a quick taste. "I might," he agreed, savoring her quick intake of breath. While her blunt questions might send him off balance, his touch upset her equilibrium. *Good to know.*

Isabella resisted the need to squirm. Leo made her hot so fast, but then he always had, ever since the first time she'd seen him with his brother Felix. Concealing her sexual yearning from him came in the difficult basket. A demanding challenge. Thank goodness she had because in her guise as a sixteen-year-old...fodder for scandal. She might cause gossip and outrage yet, if she didn't handle Leo with care.

However, her job came first. Mika had to stop his hunt. If he refused, she'd take him out. It might well be the death of her because Mika was skilled at his job, her equal as an assassin.

"If you want me, what's holding you back?" Isabella wanted to know.

The green of his eyes deepened to a jade. They glinted with amusement even though his mouth remained neutral. He knew of her desires. No doubt, the jump in her pulse when his rough tongue had slid over her skin and the rapid beat of her heart gave away her arousal. She'd need to take care, or she'd end up revealing her secrets.

He leaned back and regarded her with lazy charm. "No hurry. Plenty of good stuff between point A and B."

The air hissed between her teeth in a heated rush. *The wretch*. Why hadn't she discovered his stubborn streak earlier? She could have prepared her attack in a different manner. *Oh heck*. Who was she trying to fool?

There was no plan. She'd gone with instinct, relying on experience to tell her the right time to act.

She restrained a scowl, reaching deep for enigmatic. Assassin mode. At one hundred and fifty years old in human terms—a mere child as far as chameleons went, it was true—she was ready to retire from the assassin way of life. As soon as she took care of Mika and the associated loose ends to make sure Tomasine and Sylvie were safe, her retirement could become fact instead of a dream.

A normal life. Other assassins equated normal with boring. Isabella thought it sounded perfect.

"I'm used to fast. Instant gratification," she muttered.

His dark brows rose and unable to maintain eye contact, she stared out the window. The untamed beauty of the vivid blue waters of Wakatipu and the soaring mountain peaks surrounding the narrow lake made her heart ache. She loved the harshness of the Otago landscape, the baking-hot summer days. Even the freezing winters full of snow and sleet held their charms despite the dangers of cold to her species.

It didn't hurt that Leo Mitchell was part of the scenery. Part of her future, she hoped. Instant gratification. *Ooy*!

"Have you heard the song about a man with a slow hand?"

"Do you give all the girls this much trouble?" she demanded, hating the giveaway heat crawling through her cheeks. Isabella never blushed and found the aberration annoying. The man was a handful. He'd better be careful, or she'd shoot him. It was the way she fixed most of her problems. One bullet to the head and they faded away...

Isabella drew a deep breath and risked a glance at him. He smiled at the waitress who had arrived with a carafe of coffee. Isabella hadn't even heard her and found the fact disconcerting.

What did Leo Mitchell do when he came to Queenstown? Who did he see? He kept his romantic involvements separate from life in Middlemarch.

She'd hated knowing he saw other women but hadn't been in a position to stake a claim. Tomasine and Sylvie's safety took priority. She owed Tomasine big time. Loyalty. That was something she understood.

"I'm not trouble."

Isabella scowled, feeling the furrows form between her brows. Great. It was *her* he had an aversion to.

"Why are you frowning?" Leo asked.

His voice strummed over ruffled nerves, soothing and letting her confused mind focus. She'd start from the beginning, as if they were strangers.

"Nothing's wrong," Isabella said. "I need to contact a friend this morning. I almost forgot." They belonged together. They had loads in common.

A mission. Pretending Leo was part of another mission would make things easier to manage. She inhaled and caught a hint of the hotel's lilac soap and Leo. A shiver worked down her spine, and she grabbed her cup of coffee to avoid reaching for him. The man always smelled good. Just spending time with him smoothed away the stress churning in her belly. His enticing scent reinforced her decision to pursue. She glanced up from her coffee to find him studying her, a quizzical expression on his tanned face. She hurried into speech.

"Do you come to Queenstown often? You look familiar." And he'd be even more familiar soon. *Fingers crossed.*

Leo smiled at the waitress who delivered their meals, and Isabella had to restrain an urge to slap the woman's flirtatious grin right off her face. For a woman who'd never coveted material possessions, she felt mighty possessive toward Leo Mitchell.

Not good. Not good at all.

"More coffee?" he asked.

"Thanks." The coffee helped as a distraction, if nothing else.

Leo signaled to the other waitress, and she arrived with coffee carafe in hand along with another flirtatious grin that made Isabella's fingers grip her napkin and her thoughts turn to crime. Once the waitress left, Leo sipped his coffee, his gaze meshing with hers over the top of his cup. Instant heat prickled to life, putting her even more on edge.

"I come to Queenstown every few weeks. It's possible you've seen me here."

"Where do you live?" Isabella kept asking get-to-know-you questions to hear his voice.

"Middlemarch. It's a small town not far from Dunedin."

"I've heard of it, the Middlemarch singles dance. Don't tell me you're one of the numerous single males in search of a wife?"

Leo shrugged and drank more coffee.

Isabella upped the stakes, ready to poke the sexy kitty with a verbal stick. "No, I don't think that's it." A lie. "Don't you have something to do with vineyards?" Isabella paused as if deep in thought then clicked her fingers. "The Bunch of Grapes."

Leo's eyes narrowed. "How did you know that? Are you spying on me?" Danger lurked in his voice, his tense shoulders, and Isabella froze. Kitty prodding—not such a clever idea.

"Spying? Of course not." Fool! The Mitchells were on edge because of Tomasine, and the anxiety would be worse when someone found the body in Middlemarch. She shook her head, her throat so tight she had difficulty replying. For an experienced assassin she kept blundering around like an elephant in a tutu. *Focus, dammit.* "I saw you in the casino a few weeks ago and asked questions." Not bad. He couldn't disprove her statement.

"Why the games? Why wait until this weekend to approach me if you've seen me before?"

More questions. They'd never move into the bedroom if he maintained this dogged pace. For a male reputed to score with the ladies, he seemed on the dense side.

"A girl needs to act with caution these days. No one jumps into the first bed they see or accepts the first offer."

He snorted, his grin mocking now. "Yet that's the impression you gave last night. Didn't seem a big deal to you."

Isabella regretted her actions now. "I wasn't thinking. Could we start over and pretend we've never met before?" Isabella didn't give him an opportunity to reply, thrusting out her hand. "Hi. My name is Isabella Black. I'm pleased to meet you."

After a lengthy pause, Leo enfolded her hand in his. Warm and callused from working outdoors, the contact sent messages of lust skittering up her arm. Lord, she hoped this getting-to-know-you stuff didn't take the entire day. It felt as though they'd been having foreplay for the last year. She wanted the next step.

"Leo Mitchell." He lifted her hand to his mouth and pressed a kiss on her knuckles. His abrasive tongue sent shimmers waltzing down her spine. Easy to imagine his tongue dancing across her breasts or curling around her clit. The caresses and intoxicating sensations. She choked back a pleading moan before it could escape and embarrass her more.

"Are you all right?"

No, I'm thinking about sex. "I'm fine. Hungry though. I should eat. Where do you live in Middlemarch?"

"My family has a farm, not too far from the township." He tightened his grasp when she tugged. Her gaze flew to his, her heart lurching into a crazy beat while she waited to see what he'd do next. "Sweetheart, I've seen you in Middlemarch. Don't deny it. No more games."

Isabella fought back a sliver of fear to produce a creditable smile. "Oh, I've visited Middlemarch. I did the train trip through Tairei Gorge and spent a few hours in town. Maybe you saw me then." Heck, when had she lost control? Last night? She mocked herself, admitting the truth. Her discipline went AWOL the second Leo Mitchell walked into the casino.

"Perhaps." He appeared unconvinced.

Dangerous topic. Whenever she shifted to her Isabella guise, she kept a low profile, although she'd used the persona in Middlemarch. Other times she morphed to a male or an elderly female.

Leo set down his coffee cup. "I have an excellent memory for faces."

Sounded as if she needed to choose another face if she wanted to skulk around Middlemarch. To Isabella's relief the waitress sauntered by to ask if they needed more coffee.

"We're good," Leo said with a charming smile.

Full of jealousy, Isabella grit her teeth until the waitress drifted away. "Do you have brothers or sisters?" Her jaw ached with tension and her voice emerged husky with a serving of menace.

"I have four brothers, two older and two younger." Leo smirked, his gaze drifting to the waitress and back to her.

"Big family."

"Sometimes. It's easy to find solitude in Middlemarch, if that's what I want, but our family is close. What about you?"

Isabella envied their family vibe. Always had. She hadn't met the twins, his younger brothers, but she'd listened to stories of the numerous pranks they'd pulled while growing up. "I'm an only child. My parents died some time ago. An accident." The truth, as far as it went.

"I'm sorry to hear that. Where do you come from? You're not a New Zealander."

"I was born in Switzerland, not far from the Italian border. My parents moved around for my father's work." Assassins tended to move around. It kept them alive.

"What do you do for a job?"

Ah, the question she'd wanted to avoid. Funny how people always asked the same questions. Where do you live? What do you do? They used the answers to slot new acquaintances into neat pigeonholes, to discover where they came on the social scale. "When I'm not playing tourist, I work in hotels. Anything from receptionist to bartender."

Leo nodded. "Would you still like to spend the day with me?"

"What did you have in mind?" Although sex was uppermost in her thoughts, she'd take whatever was on offer.

"I need to check in at the Bunch of Grapes to sign paperwork, but the rest of the day is mine. I mentioned a picnic last night. How does that sound? We could go swimming."

"I don't have a swimsuit."

"Shame." His voice slid into intimate, flustering her.

51

She sucked in a hasty breath. "Um...a picnic sounds great, but I can't leave until after eleven thirty. I have a job interview." The fabricated excuse gave her leeway in case something went wrong during the meeting with Mika. Oh yes. A picnic. Perfect...anything to get him alone.

"I'll meet you in the lobby after your interview. Say twelve?"

"Twelve it is." Isabella frowned at the rashers of bacon on her plate, instinct telling her she couldn't count on surrender from Leo. She needed to pull back, let him set the pace or she'd lose him. But surely, he wasn't going to keep resisting? She'd hate to use force, but if he continued to tease, Isabella could see coercion in the future.

On replaying the thought, a shiver of distaste rippled through her. Good grief. Deranged—from frustration and Leo-induced stress or maybe her mother had been right in her claim that the life of an assassin sucked away humanity. According to her, an assassin eventually became soulless, incapable of feeling, of love. Those had been her dying words. After her mother had shot Isabella's father in the head and left him in a pool of black, sticky blood.

She was *not* an empty husk and refused to end up like her parents. Yes, excluding an accident she'd have a long life and accepted Leo would die before her. After many happy years together, if she had her way. A lasting relationship with Leo was her objective, not just sex. *Although she could handle lust.*

Isabella wanted a partnership with Leo Mitchell.

No other man would do.

Chapter 4

Picnic Seduction

I sabella watched Leo surreptitiously while he drove through the Kawarau Gorge toward the vineyards, pleased her business with Mika had gone well. Relaxed in the knowledge Mika was en route to Auckland, she turned her attention to the scenery.

Below the curling road, the Kawarau River snaked between boulders, the ferocious force of the water carving a path past huge blocks of granite. Names like Roaring Meg hinted at the gold history in the area, as did the tourist attraction with its old mining equipment and makeshift shanty huts. Heat scored the countryside, giving it a dry and barren appearance, but come the spring wildflowers blazed bright pink, white and yellow on these hills and along the roadside.

Traffic was heavy, and they passed several buses loaded with tourists. Unsurprising since Queenstown was the adventure capital of New Zealand, and eager tourists flocked there to scare themselves silly while trying new extreme sports.

"How long are you spending in New Zealand?" he asked.

"I have no set plans," Isabella said. "I'm enjoying it here. Hopefully, I get the job." As long as it takes.

"Let me know," Leo said. "I have a few contacts if you don't get this one. What was it?"

"Thanks. A bartender position." Isabella tried to sound grateful even though he peeved her with his nonchalant offer. Didn't he want her to stay? Didn't he realize they were fated mates? She'd known from the moment he'd walked into Tomasine's rented house, even though it was unusual for chameleons to mate with other shifters. She'd suffered ever since.

Ten minutes later, they pulled up outside a building marked *Staff Only*. Before reaching the vineyard entrance, they'd passed rows of grapevines. Each row had a rosebush planted at the end, the apricot-colored flowers providing a nice touch. The striking buildings, comprising of a tasting room, cellar and restaurant grabbed attention. The curved walls and soaring roof reminded Isabella of a huge bird in flight. She recalled Emily and Saber discussing the vineyard buildings winning awards for original design. It was easy to see why.

Leo glanced at his watch. "I need to check in at the office. The shop and cellar area are open if you want to browse while you're waiting. I won't be long. I promise." He smiled, and to her astonishment, pressed a quick kiss on her lips before climbing from the SUV and striding away to disappear through a white door.

She blinked when the door swung shut, cutting off his image. A throaty sigh filled the SUV interior. A sexy image. His hunter-green polo shirt hugged his chest, highlighting the muscular frame beneath, and his black shorts clung to his backside. Leo Mitchell packed a sensual punch, one she had no remedy against. One look and her heart raced, her body softening while her mind pondered possibilities. Despite her mother's warnings, she intended to pursue a relationship. It was possible for a chameleon to have a life. A happy life.

Her fingers crept up to caress her mouth and she rubbed them across her lips. Maybe things were progressing slower than she preferred, but he'd kissed her of his own free will. Things were looking up.

"Who's the woman?" Chase asked.

Leo scowled a warning as he strode across the tile floor of the office to join his shifter friend where he stood by the desk. They stared out of the window and watched Isabella climb from his vehicle. She stretched and Chase whistled in admiration.

"That's my mate," Leo said in sharp warning. His gaze drifted to Isabella's long, tanned legs, displayed to perfection in brief shorts. "Hands off. Dammit, eyes too. She's mine."

Chase tilted his head, his green eyes twinkling with devilry. "Does she know?"

"Stay away." Leo growled a warning deep in his throat and bared his teeth. The hair at the scruff of his neck prickled and lifted in a territorial catlike manner. "We haven't discussed the finer details but I intend to. Today."

Chase laughed and backed away, his hands raised in a gesture of surrender. "Man, I can take a hint. Personally, I prefer blondes."

"If I find any, I'll send them your way," Leo said, still eyeing his friend with suspicion. Dammit, he couldn't pussyfoot around any longer. Isabella was offering. He wanted. So this time he was gonna take, even if he wasn't sure what to make of the mystery woman. Trust. That was another issue, but the urges thrumming through his mind and body beat like a jungle drum. Another growl rattled in his throat and a feral grin crawled across his lips. By the time he finished, she'd crave him, not another male. "Where's the paperwork I need to take care of?"

"Over here." Chase dropped onto the chair behind the cluttered wooden desk.

Leo took a seat opposite, accepted a sheaf of papers and read the supplier contract requiring a signature. He checked a press release for an upcoming fashion show they were holding at the vineyard and scanned the guest list. "Looks good, Chase. Is that it for today or do you need me to do something else?"

"Go claim your mate. I can take care of anything that comes up."

"Yeah. I know you can. Thanks." Leo stood, and with a wave headed out to find Isabella.

He found her flirting with the two men looking after the wine tasting for the day. Figured. The woman attracted attention wherever she went. Part of him puffed up with pride while the feline inside resented other men looking.

"Have you tried any of our wine?" he asked, walking up behind her and sliding a possessive arm around her waist. His measured stare at the two men didn't go unheeded. They became all business, one leaving to help other tourists and the remaining pouring a small sample of one of their award-winning Pinot Noir wines into a glass for Isabella. He nodded at Leo and left them alone.

"Excellent wine." Isabella twirled the glass in her hand and held it up to study the rich ruby color.

"You ready to go?"

"Anytime," she purred.

Leo's groin tightened. She meant something else and they both knew it. The woman had a wicked mouth. He couldn't wait to experience it wrapped around his dick. "Good," he said. "Let's do it."

He felt her shock rather than saw it and had difficulty restraining his bark of laughter, but he came to a decision. He'd take her word regarding the other man she'd kissed in the

Queenstown casino—give her the benefit of the doubt—and let things progress.

Leo knew she was his mate, sensed it deep in his gut. Her non-shifter status didn't matter. His brothers would approve and welcome a woman—even a human—to their family if it meant he'd decided to grow up and act with maturity. No more shenanigans to turn Saber's hair gray and upset the members of the council. Sure, as a randy teenager, he'd fantasized of running free with his mate, another black leopard, but he could run with his brothers whenever the urge struck.

"I'll grab the picnic basket from the SUV."

"Are we walking far?"

"Far enough to guarantee privacy." This time Leo caught the rounded O of surprise before her mouth smoothed out and her face blanked. Good. He'd hate to think he was predictable. He opened the back of his vehicle and pulled out the square straw basket Erin had packed for them. After slamming the rear door, he turned to Isabella. "We need to walk through the vineyard."

Isabella fell into step beside him. She kept glancing at him when she didn't think he'd notice. Her looks held confusion and longing. It was the yearning that twisted his insides into knots of anticipation. He wondered if it were possible to muck up a mating, if it were possible to mate with the wrong woman. The twins had asked Saber the same thing. Saber hadn't known. He'd said each mating was different. Each couple had a different journey to complete. His answer hadn't been very illuminating then and now the knowledge, or lack of, didn't sit any easier. The mating process seemed bloody complicated.

They strolled between the rows of vines and the sounds of traffic and visitors to the vineyard receded. A companionable silence fell between them. Once they were through the vines, Leo followed the fence, leading the way. He sensed her gaze on his back, and the knowledge played havoc with his wayward body. He scowled at his erection. Damn cock had developed a mind of its own.

He stopped halfway along the fence line. "We need to climb over the fence. Do you need a hand?"

Isabella took hold of a post and vaulted over. "No. I'm good."

Leo gaped and snapped his mouth shut. It took upper body strength to emulate Isabella's action. Suddenly, he couldn't wait to explore her sleek muscles.

He handed her the basket of food and jumped over the fence to land at her side. "I'll take that. Follow the path running alongside the stream." He indicated the direction with a jerk of his head and stood back to let her take the lead.

Torture. The sway of her pert backside was pure torture, yet he couldn't tear away his gaze. Another ten minutes passed and Leo decided on a swim the minute they reached the waterfall, so great was the heat crawling across his skin.

It took another fifteen minutes of walking before he heard the rush of water as it raced over the craggy granite rocks and spilled into the pool beneath. They rounded the corner and he took the lead, pushing past a green bushy fern and onto a different path.

The falls were in front of them. Huge rocks littered the riverbed like a giant's marbles, blocking the flow of the water and creating a pool suitable for swimming. Trees and ferns surrounded the small clearing they'd entered.

Leo set the basket under a tree and tugged out the tartan rug Erin had packed in the top. He spread it out so it was partially in the shade and stood. His gaze settled on Isabella's face. She swallowed, appearing wary. Leo whipped his shirt over his head and tossed it aside. He slid off his sandals and grinned. Her eyes widened when he prowled closer.

He regarded her in a quizzical manner. "Don't tell me you've changed your mind."

"About what?"

"Being here with me."

"No."

Leo noticed the way her gaze skittered over his torso and grazed his groin before meandering to his face.

"I...what are you doing?"

"Going for a swim. Coming in?" Leo enjoyed the hesitation, the wariness in her expression so much that he decided to push her in the same manner she'd goaded him last night. He tugged off his shorts and stepped free of them before swaggering down the sloping bank to reach the water.

Once again, he sensed her ogling him. His cock jumped, his body singing with lust. Hell, he wouldn't be surprised if the water bubbled and steam shrouded the clearing when he hit the pool. He waded into the water, listening intently, trying to discern her reaction. He dove under and the coolness barely made a dent on the heat searing his skin. The need to claim her pounded him, bringing determination and confidence.

This was the right thing to do. He was certain of it.

The trust and getting to know her could come later. He'd claim her first then take care of the rest at leisure. He surfaced with a surging leap and turned to see if Isabella had moved.

She stood stock-still, a frown marring her striking features. "Is it deep? I can't swim," she called over the flow of the water.

"It comes up to my chest at the deepest part," he shouted. "Come in and I'll give you a swimming lesson." *Among other things.*

"Do you promise not to dunk me under the water?"

"Cross my heart."

Isabella hesitated for a fraction longer before kicking off her leather sandals. "Is it cold?"

"No. Should I provide music?" he called.

Isabella gave a rude snort. "I need to have a few drinks before I can play the stripper. Close your eyes."

"But the scenery is so enticing." The contrast between wanton and shy brought the need to smile. "Besides, you watched me. Fair turnabout."

"Wretch."

"I heard that," he protested.

"You must have superb hearing."

"My eyesight is excellent too."

"Of course it is," she retorted, all sweetness and light. "But I'm sure you have faults." She cocked her head, bringing a swift impression of a curious bird. "Yeah, your ears look on the big side."

Leo chuckled. "Other parts of me are big as well." Fascinated, he watched a delicate pink collect in her cheeks. Even after her brazen approach the previous night, he'd embarrassed her with his frank talk. The contrasts intrigued him, making him want to dig below the surface to discover what made the woman tick.

"I have your word for that," she retorted.

Leo laughed and took a step toward the bank. The water level reduced, exposing his body from head to belly. If she looked hard enough, she'd see the shadow of his erection because the cool mountain water wasn't denting his libido. Nope, just one look at the curvy woman hesitating on the bank brought heady desire and a raging hard-on. He took another step toward her, leaving no doubt as to his size.

Isabella gasped and half turned away.

He sprang from the water, his heart pounding with the thrill of the chase. She could run if she liked but he'd catch her. She didn't stand a chance.

"Isabella." She halted with her back to him, but Leo noticed the faint tremor of her limbs.

"Yes?"

"We don't know each other but you can trust me. Say no, and I'll respect your wishes." *Even if her on-again, off-again reactions confused the hell out of him.* Something told him she was just as confused as he.

"I don't want to say no," she whispered.

As he watched, she swallowed and unfastened the top button of her sky-blue shirt. When he didn't move, she undid the next. Leo held his breath. Two more to go before the shirt gaped wide enough to display her breasts. Last night hadn't been enough. No this time, he wanted a long, leisurely look followed by touching. Lots of touching.

The third button separated from the hole and the blue fabric fell away from her breasts, revealing pale golden skin and shadowed cleavage along with a blue bra, a shade or two lighter than her shirt. Her hands fell to her sides, jerking Leo's gaze to her face.

"Is that it?" he demanded. "A little skin? I've gone all the way for you."

"Looks as if you sunbathe all the way," she said, her tone dry.

"I thought you'd copped a look." Leo didn't bother to hide his smugness. He liked teasing her and loved her unpredictable behavior even though it had the potential to drive him crazy.

"I did. Do I appear stupid? Dull-witted?"

Leo grunted but stood relaxed in front of her, or as relaxed as he could be with an erection and a beautiful woman within touching distance. She looked anything but stupid. The glint of shrewd intelligence in her eyes was part of her attraction and the perfection of her form didn't hurt one bit. But it was the shy, elusive quality that did it for him.

63

This morning he hadn't been sure he was doing the right thing, but now she'd tossed a silent challenge. His head tilted a fraction to the side to watch her. "Want to touch?"

"Yes."

The blunt honesty revved him. A shot of electricity flared across his skin. His cock jerked, lengthening to painful. Leo attempted to concentrate on Isabella. He cleared his throat. "Come touch me then. I won't bite." Not much, as long as he could control himself. He hadn't indulged in a round of sweaty sex for the last three months. Oh, his body had been eager but his mind refused a woman who wasn't his mate. Now at last body and mind reconciled. Time to take this thing simmering between them to its natural conclusion.

Isabella huffed out a quick breath. Damn, she wanted to touch, but fear of the consequences held her back, jerked her from character. She gave herself a hard mental shake, trying to dispel the stupid nerves that had appeared from nowhere. Any of her assassin acquaintances seeing her in this namby-pamby mood would laugh themselves hoarse. Talk about a ninny. Isabella Black never had doubts. She made a decision and went with it. Always. It was part of her nature—before she shifted to a new persona, she calculated each behavioral trait and stuck to type while in the role. She never deviated, never gave less than one hundred percent because attention to detail meant life trumped death. This quiver of nerves shocked her speechless.

"Go on. I dare you."

Isabella shot him a flirtatious look, or at least she intended flirty. She suspected she projected an irritated sparkle rather than playful and enticing. Oh, she wanted to touch, but the truth resonated within her. If she failed in this relationship with Leo, if he rejected her, she'd lose everything.

Everything.

A sobering thought, and one that made her dither.

Soft. During her stay in Middlemarch she'd become lax. Must be something in the air. Middlemarch and contact with the Mitchell family changed people, had changed her.

"Isabella. *Isabella.*" Warm hands closed around her biceps, the touch searing through her body like wildfire on the drought-stricken Canterbury Plains. Her head jerked upward, panic riding her hard. Her heart thudded erratically. A deep breath did nothing to ease the charge of fear. Instead, she dragged in his enticing scent along with a hit of the great outdoors. Greenery. Damp moss. Moist dirt. Feline male.

"You were miles away. I think I should be offended," he added in a dry tone. "I'm naked and you go off into a daydream." A rakish smile curved his lips without warning. "Unless I starred in your dreams." He rubbed a thumb across her lips. "That I'd find acceptable."

Isabella suppressed a tremor of awareness at his closeness. If she looked down, she'd get a good eyeful of his cock. Heat emanated from his skin, even though her sole contact was thumb to lips. For an instant longer apprehension held her immobile then her breath eased out in a steady whoosh. She couldn't stay in the form of Gina for the rest of her life. Change—it was good and necessary.

Throwing caution to the Otago winds, she stepped into his personal space, bringing their bodies together in decadent contact. How could anything this good be wrong? She clutched Leo's powerful shoulders and raised her head for a kiss.

Leo shook his head, his green eyes narrowing. "I don't get you. You're confusing. I want you. I admit it, but I'm not into games. If you're trying to play me...all I can say is don't."

Great. She'd almost screwed up the best thing that had ever happened to her with her namby-pamby behavior. *Get a grip, Isabella.*

His displeasure came through crisp and clear. If she didn't do something, she'd lose him. Her fish would jump the hook, leaving her with tall fisherman tales to tell in her old age. Assuming she didn't die on the job meantime.

After another deep breath, Isabella attempted honesty, or as much as she dared for the time being. "I'm not playing games. I'm not a fan of them myself. The truth is I've noticed you before in the casino. I wanted to be the woman with you...instead of the others I'd seen dangling off your arm. I decided on brazen behavior to grab your attention. It's more difficult than I thought because I'm not audacious at heart." Her heart pitter-pattered while she waited for his reaction.

Smoke and screens. She was skilled at them. Half-truths were natural, but each lie to Leo and his family jabbed her conscience. She'd grown scruples. A sad state of affairs for an assassin.

Leo cupped her face with his hands, his warm breath on her skin bringing a ripple of delight. "Sweetheart, I liked the brazen, but what I want is the real you. Be yourself, that's all I ask."

He didn't know what he asked. She scowled while pondering her dilemma. Best not worry about the future. No, she'd take each day one at a time.

"I think I can do that," she whispered.

The twinkle in his eyes faded to serious, and his hands fell to rest on her shoulders. "Should I get dressed?"

Isabella hesitated before leaping into the unknown. "I don't think so. I am warm after the trek here." And his touch wasn't helping to cool the spike of heat rushing through her body.

"You going to swim?" Surprise flickered across his face followed by delight. "That's great. I have to warn you. I lied about the water temperature. It's bloody freezing."

"Might help you." Isabella gave his groin a pointed glance. As for her, the chilly water might jolt commonsense into her Leo-soaked brain. That couldn't be a bad thing...as long as she took care and didn't stay in too long.

"A kiss first."

The words were so soft she strained to hear. Then blood rushed through her head along with excitement. "Yes."

"Good to hear we're in agreement." With a gleeful smile, he leaned in and pressed his lips to hers, as if he were afraid she'd take fright and run.

Isabella relaxed and let her breasts brush his bare chest. Her nipples pulled tight, and the move diverted the kiss from innocent. She gasped at the added sensations, new and exciting and better than scenarios her imagination conjured. Leo took control, nibbling at her bottom lip and pushing his tongue against hers. Their breaths mingled. His flavor rolled over her, rubbing away the last of her reticence.

Her hands crept around behind his neck to anchor herself. Yes, this was what she needed, had dreamed of during long lonely nights.

Leo drew her closer still, pressing their bodies together from mouth to groin, but to her surprise, his hands didn't wander. Although they touched, Leo confined his attentions to the kiss. His tongue thrust into her mouth, bringing an ache that settled in her pussy. With each stroke of his tongue, hot, sensual flames licked across her flesh. Isabella trembled, the reality of being in Leo's arms even better than her imagination. Damn, she could feel his touch clear to her toes. Dampness gathered at the juncture of her thighs, her intimate flesh becoming slick. Swollen. Needy.

Finally Leo pulled back to scan her face. He grinned and leaned close again to press his forehead against hers. Isabella sighed and wondered if her heart rate would settle to something resembling normal.

Leo pushed his hands against her shoulders, winked at her and settled in to kiss her again. The warm, wet suction against her bottom lip brought a jolt of heat to her core, a rush of juices. His lips covered hers again and her vagina fluttered. Arousal spiraled low, pushing at her control. She wanted more, needed it. Her fingers smoothed through the hair at his nape and tugged to get his attention.

"Ow, woman." Leo broke their kiss to stare at her. "Is there a problem?"

"Too much kissing."

His mouth dropped open. "Haven't you heard of foreplay?"

Foreplay? Isabella refrained from scoffing but let loose in her mind. Foreplay? Hell, since first clapping eyes on Leo Mitchell she'd suffered through foreplay, fantasizing and everything in between. Oh yeah, she'd suffered.

"I haven't had sex for a long time. This time I don't need a lot of foreplay. Besides, it doesn't look as though you need it either."

"I like the bit that comes before. Just because my body is ready doesn't mean I don't enjoy touching and holding you. Kissing." A touch of indignation colored his tone, and Isabella knew she needed to step warily. She didn't want to scare him off. On the other hand, he'd have trouble squeezing back into his form-fitting shorts in that state. Her lips twitched in the beginnings of an evil grin.

"Are you laughing at me?" he demanded without warning.

"No." Isabella's lips twitched harder and a laugh burst free.

"You little witch. You are laughing." He maintained a sober expression but devilment glittered in his eyes.

Isabella took an unsteady step back, positive the look meant trouble. On her second retreating step, she stumbled over a rock. As a chameleon, she was quick, but today she needed to factor in clumsiness. With the unfair advantage, Leo moved faster. Before she knew it, he'd scooped her off her feet and held her in his arms.

"Leo, put me down."

"Woman, you've been pushing me since the moment I found you in my bed. It's time I gained the upper hand."

"I'll behave. Promise. You take the lead during sex since it seems important to you."

He halted and glared at her. "I should take your word on that?"

"You should! Leo, please put me down."

He strode toward the pool at the base of the fall, ignoring her protests.

"You can't throw me in. I don't have any dry clothes." She had to ease into cold.

"You should have thought of that before." He waded into the water and despite her frantic wriggling, Isabella found his strength too great for her. Seconds later icy water soaked into her clothes, and Leo let her go.

She went under, the water even colder than Leo indicated. She surged from the water, coming up with a screech, the icy temperature working against her chameleon genes. Her teeth chattered uncontrollably and she knew she'd need to warm up now. She waded for the bank. Uncoordinated hands attempted to unbutton her sodden shorts and tug them down her legs. She took two tries to unfasten the button on the fly closure. Trembling fingers managed the zipper and the shorts loosened, the material falling to her feet, helped by gravity.

Isabella was vaguely aware of Leo clambering from the pool but worried more about getting warm. Thank goodness the sun shone overhead. If she stripped and wrapped herself in the blanket, her body heat should rise. She hadn't been immersed for long. Normally it was okay because she never exposed herself to sudden extremes of temperature. Dunked rated as sudden.

"Are you okay?" Concern filled Leo's voice and his hands settled on her shoulders. He turned her to face him, all traces of humor dropping away when he saw the way her teeth chattered. He felt the icy chill of her skin and sprang into action. "Let's get these clothes off. I have a towel." He released her long enough to retrieve an orange-and-purple beach towel from the picnic basket.

Despite the sun, a shiver racked her body. The fabric of her shirt, plastered against her skin like a cold compress, exacerbated the intense chill. Her fingers refused to work and her legs turned to jelly, unwilling to hold her weight. With a soft cry, she toppled over, the world going black.

Chapter 5

A Claiming

"Isabella?"

Horror filled Leo when she crumpled. He sprang to her side and crouched beside her. What the fuck? Her skin prickled with icy chills. The water hadn't been that cold. Immersed for mere seconds, she should be fine. He checked her pulse. Faint and thready, it alarmed the hell out of him.

Leo yanked off her remaining clothes, trying to be gentle despite his worry. Once he'd stripped her, he grabbed the towel and dried her off, rubbing firmly to get her circulation moving. Not much warmer, and he couldn't understand why. He tugged the rug into the direct sunshine and wrapped it around her. Part of the local Middlemarch Search and Rescue team, he decided he'd dry off and try to warm her with his own body heat. If that didn't work, he'd ring Chase and get him to drive through the vineyards to meet them.

Leo rubbed the damp towel over his body and hair, blotting away the worst of the water. Casting it aside, he unwrapped Isabella and curled up beside her before covering them both.

"Isabella?" he whispered.

The lack of a reply worried him but at least her pulse beat stronger. He drew her into his arms, wincing at her frozen skin. A few minutes. That was all he'd give her. If she didn't respond, he'd contact Chase and they'd put her in a hot bath until medical help arrived.

He rubbed his hands over her back. Her soft groan brought relief.

"Isabella?"

Her eyelids fluttered and he glimpsed her eyes. A weird silver color. Leo blinked.

"Hi," he whispered. "How are you? You gave me a fright." Worry had made him see things. Her eyes were their normal sexy mix of blue and violet.

"What happened?" Confusion puckered her brow.

"I tossed you in the pool and you collapsed."

Isabella avoided his gaze. "I'm not good with cold."

"But you come from Switzerland."

"I dress for it and spend most of the winter indoors, hovering near the open fire."

Indoors. Open Fire. Leo's mind darted straight to sex. It didn't help that his naked body plastered against hers from chest to groin. Even their legs tangled together, and it felt every bit as good as he'd imagined.

73

"I won't make the mistake of tossing you in a mountain stream again. Why didn't you say something?"

"I didn't realize the water temperature...normally, I submerge myself gradually."

"I tossed you in. Hell, I'm sorry." Leo forced himself to peel away from her body, noting she felt warmer already. "I'm afraid your clothes are soaked. I didn't think to spread them out to dry. Wrap up in the blanket until we get back to the vineyard, and I can find you dry clothes."

Isabella sat up and allowed the blanket to fall away. It pooled around her waist, baring her breasts. The delicate pink nipples pulled tight with the cold.

Leo glanced away, but the vision had seared to his retinas. She was beautiful, even better than he'd imagined with sleek, muscular grace. He hadn't taken the time to have a good look while he'd undressed her, too worried about her slip into unconsciousness.

"I'm fine. Don't treat me like an invalid."

"You were unconscious."

"I'm not now. Do you have something sweet to eat in the picnic basket?"

"Probably," Leo said.

"Good. Then that's all I need to get my blood sugars up again. If you have coffee—that will help too."

Leo studied her. She appeared better now with a sparkle in her eyes. After a brief hesitation, he decided she knew best. He stood and strode to the picnic basket. When he checked the contents, he found two portions of rich chocolate gateaux. That should do the trick. He pulled it out plus a spoon and returned to Isabella's side. She'd arranged the rug to screen her body. Too late. He'd already had a good look.

"Here you go." After he opened the plastic container, he held out the dessert and spoon, knowing Isabella would need to loosen her hold on the blanket in order to eat. Difficult to rake up the faintest hint of guilt when he couldn't wait to stare at her luscious body again. "Eat as much as you need. I don't mind sacrificing my portion for a good cause."

Somehow, Isabella rearranged the blanket and accepted the gateaux without a hitch. While he watched, she dug into the dessert and lifted a spoonful to her mouth. Her eyes closed as she savored the bite. A faint moan emerged. Fascinated, he couldn't take his gaze off her. He watched her swallow, saw her tongue rasp against a piece of icing sticking to the spoon. She spooned more into her mouth, the sheer carnality of the move and the tiny sounds of appreciation jolting his body to full awareness.

"Are you going to share?" The husky cadence of his voice grabbed her attention.

Her brows arched. "Do you want some?"

Oh yeah, baby. Big time, but for now he'd have to make do with gateaux.

"Please." Leo stilled, panic stirring inside. Every muscle tightened, his bones ached, his body instructing him to shift. A fine time for his feline senses to tell him to pounce. The cherry on his day. After sending his date into an unconscious state, he turned feral and jumped her. They'd hear her screech of horror in Middlemarch if he gave in to the impulse to shift to cat.

He strained for control, a fine tremor passing through his muscles. He sucked in a deep breath and gave his feline a mental push. *Down kitty*.

"Here you go."

Leo glanced up to see a spoonful of gateaux float in front of him. Instinctively he opened his mouth and closed his lips around the sweet confection. His pulse jumped like a startled rabbit when the chocolate flooded his taste buds. His gaze met hers and he was lost.

Leo pounced.

Not even her startled *eek* stopped his charge. The spoon dropped and clattered against a small rock. Chocolate oozed between their bodies, the gateaux decorating his belly. Thankfully, he didn't shift, but it was a close thing. He felt the distinct prickle of skin that foretold the glossy pelt of black and dark claws formed in place of his fingernails. Her smooth skin beneath his fingertips tested his control issues.

Kiss her senseless. Keep her busy while—hopefully—he could multitask and restrain his feline. Clasping her more tightly, he lowered his head and staked a claim. Their lips mashed together before they found the perfect fit.

She plunged her fingers into his hair. Their lips and tongues moved together.

Leo relaxed a fraction, and settled in to extract maximum pleasure from the close physical contact. With care, he tugged the blanket away to expose her breasts to his gaze. Rounded. Not too big, but not too small either, he could imagine cupping them in his hands, savoring the warm weight of her.

His tongue slid between her lips, the decadent flavor of chocolate dancing across his senses. In the past he hadn't appreciated the healthful benefits of chocolate. Now...now he might have to change his mind. Gradually he lowered her to the ground and covered her with his larger body. Her soft groan of pain reminded him they were lying on the hard sunbaked ground. He rolled without parting their lips so he ended up on the bottom with sweet Isabella plastered on top.

Sweet yet sexy. The woman combined innocence and plain sex siren, calling his feline to play. Although the cat had ceased pushing for release, the faint shadow of claws still showed through his fingernails. Losing control concerned him but one thing was certain—the first time they had sex would be explosive. And he knew which position they'd be using—one where he had a great view but Isabella didn't. It was that or a blindfold. Hmmm, possibilities.

Isabella pulled her lips away from his and stared at him in an impish manner. "I was enjoying that dessert. Now it's plastered over our stomachs."

"I can fix that easily enough." Leo licked his lips. Gently, he pushed her off his body and rolled to his feet. He grasped her hand and tugged her to her feet, pleased she'd recovered from her dip in the water. "Are you sure you're all right? Should we head back to Queenstown?"

"No!" Panic struck Isabella. No way. No how. Somehow she had to seduce him before she went mad. She needed sex, dammit. Frustration simmered through her mind while a faint chill still eddied through her limbs, a remnant of the icy water. Heck, the man probably thought she was a sandwich short of a picnic. What kind of woman fainted when chucked into a waterhole on a hot and sunny day?

A weird look crossed his face. "Are you pregnant?"

"No, I am not pregnant." She couldn't have children with anyone but another chameleon. No chance of that when her race was almost extinct. "I resent the implication." *Go, Leo. Way to kill the mood.*

Leo's brows drew together in a frown. "Why are you so keen to sleep with me?"

"Hello? Have you looked in a mirror? You're gorgeous. I'm in lust and wanted to get to know you. No sinister motives. I'm not pregnant and don't intend falling pregnant."

An opportunity to tell him she couldn't have children but she didn't take it. The inability to have children made her feel less—a shaming secret to keep close and let others know on a need-to basis. Such as a prospective mate or husband. They were nowhere near that place, not when they hadn't even had sex.

She sucked in a deep breath. "Besides, I'm on birth control pills." *Liar.* Isabella had to stop herself from reaching for her nose to check if it had grown.

"Sorry. Women have tried to trick me in the past and sometimes I think the worst of people."

"I promise I'm not trying to trap you. Besides, it's not as if I intend to hang around New Zealand forever. Eventually I'll head home." Another lie but worth it since the tension left his expression.

The sexy male stalked across to the blanket she'd left in a heap on the ground. Beautifully naked, he wasn't the slightest bit self-conscious. She took her cue from him and pretended being naked in the outdoors with a sexy male at hand was no big deal. Her libido, however, had other ideas. Her breasts tingled while moisture gathered at her folds. A hungry ache sprang to life with each flex of his muscles.

He spread out the blanket in a soft and shady spot before retrieving something from inside the basket. When he tossed the object on the blanket, she saw it was a strip of condoms.

Isabella bit back a moan while a jolt of pleasure zapped straight to her clit. It had been so long since a man had touched her. Living undercover robbed her of the opportunity, and once she'd seen Leo, that was it—no one else would suffice.

"Come here."

Isabella's brain told her feet to obey and she stood in front of him. Six inches taller than her, he glanced down in faint challenge. A trace of color highlighted his cheekbones. His green eyes glinted, and she'd have to be blind not to notice his cock. Thick and swollen, it thrust upward, grazing his chocolate-covered stomach.

With a quivering hand, she reached out to grasp his biceps. Smooth, sun-warmed skin greeted her touch while up close his natural musky scent with the hint of chocolate did things to her hormones. She bit on her bottom lip, uncertain of how to proceed.

Without warning, Leo scooped her off her feet, cradling her in his arms. "No more playing," he drawled. "I'm going to make love to you. If you want me to stop, now's the time to say so."

"No, I—"

"No?" Disappointment blazed across his face and infused his voice.

"I mean yes," Isabella blurted. "What I meant to say was, no, I don't want you to stop, and yes, we should make love right now before an avalanche or some other disaster strikes."

"Good point." He chuckled as he lowered her to the blanket. "So far our relationship makes me think of a set of traffic lights stuck on short phase."

"Great simile." Isabella stared up at him, drowning in his compelling gaze. He seemed tense, his smile fixed. She knew the off-balance sensation—sort of like stepping off a cliff. "Fate chuckles at our expense."

"Yeah." His hand grazed one breast. She gasped, and he grinned, the tense set leaving his shoulders. Gently, he cupped her cheek and pressed a kiss to the tip of her nose. "Let's see if I can make you purr."

Isabella knew he meant it in the feline sense even though he assumed she was a human. The chameleon, being an old and evolved species, could fool anyone with its disguises. He would never smell her otherness, even with his acute feline senses. Not unless she willed otherwise. Yeah, purring she could do.

The first swipe of his tongue across her belly was so delicate she almost didn't register it. The second, more pronounced, rasped across her skin to clean off the gateaux that had transferred from his stomach to hers.

Her toes curled and her eyes fluttered shut to concentrate on the sensations. His tongue circled her bellybutton and dipped inside. She relaxed into the blanket, content for the first time in months. He lapped her skin, cleaning off the chocolate in the most decadent, sexy manner she'd ever experienced. Gradually he worked to her mound.

She fidgeted, arousal swelling within her. With the silent pressure of his hands, he requested her to part her legs and allow him to settle between. It was all Isabella could do to bite back a moan of pleasure. Each breath emerged in a ragged gasp, her pulse raced way out of control, her skin now toasty warm. Clawing tension took possession of her body. If he stopped now, she'd have to hurt him. Not even the fear of explaining to Saber Mitchell of how and why she'd hurt his younger brother could stop her.

"You're gorgeous. Sexy."

"Then why did you send me away last night," she fired back, opening her eyes to glare.

"I choose my women. I'm not a hunk of meat." The words simmered between them, holding a hint of accusation.

Isabella frowned, getting his point. Bother, her smart comment had halted proceeds. If she didn't shut up, he'd leave. "I'm attracted to you. Yes, you're pretty, but it's easy to see you're more than the product of a good gene pool. I'm sorry if I've given you a different impression." Maybe if she laid it on thick enough, his thoughts would return to sex. She writhed against him.

"Humph." Leo's masculine displeasure remained clear. "Don't think your feminine wiles will distract me."

Isabella ran her hand over his shoulder and refrained from meeting his gaze. She'd bet her feminine wiles over his stubbornness any day. Once she unleashed her full sensual arsenal, the poor baby wouldn't stand a chance. Her fingers trailed over a pectoral muscle. She repeated the move, this time letting her fingernails dig into the taut flesh. He grunted and moved a fraction to give her better access.

With the chill in her body dissipated, the scare behind her, Isabella concentrated on Leo and his scrumptious torso. They would have sex, dammit, before they left this picnic spot. Determined, she pushed him off her, and before he could move away, she straddled his waist, pinning the stubborn male in place. She wasn't about to allow anyone to distract her from this self-imposed mission.

Isabella moved down his body, smiling when she felt the prod of his cock on her backside. She lifted her body and maneuvered so she sat on his upper thighs and had access to his working parts. A wicked grin curved her lips. Functioning parts soon.

"Isabella?"

"Yeah?" She licked her lips, wondering where to kiss and nuzzle first.

"Get off me."

Isabella gaped, freezing in place. "Huh?"

"Off." His hands dug into her thighs, pushing insistently.

"But why? I thought—"

"You have no idea what I'm thinking, but for the record, I'm the male. Let me take control."

Huh? Isabella couldn't get past the shock holding her in its grip. Things had been going so well.

"Better close your mouth, sweetheart, before a nasty insect flies inside." He used his finger to tap her mouth.

Scowling, Isabella climbed off, but before she could decide whether to stalk off indignantly or rip into him, he grasped her upper arms and pushed her onto the blanket. The air crackled with tension when they stared at each other. He smiled, his eyes full of tenderness.

"Please, for once, no games. Just let me lead this dance." He moved before she could form a reply, his lips sealing in her indignation. Her irritation faded under the onslaught of his touch, his talented lips and fingers. His fingers drifted across her collarbone. The nip of teeth made her start, but the rasp of his tongue soothed the sting.

She relaxed again, giving herself over to his magic touch. Maybe he was right. Maybe she had control issues.

SHELLEY MUNRO

"Relax. That's it." He exhaled against her neck, the warm puff of air wringing a shiver from her that echoed low in her belly. He flexed his body against her hip, the brush of his cock leaving a damp trail.

Burning up inside, she willed him to hurry. The warm, wet suction against her neck would leave a mark. The idea made her shiver. Again. She liked the idea of bearing his mark of passion. A pity it would disappear when she shifted.

"Put your arms above your head and leave them there until I tell you to move."

"I'll seize up."

"By the time I'm finished with you, you'll be melting like a puddle of warm butter. You'll be so sated you won't feel a thing."

"Promises, promises."

"I never break a promise," he said in his husky voice.

The truth. She knew this from firsthand experience. The memory made her release the last bit of tension pushing at her mind. She sighed and gave herself into his keeping, trusting him to keep her safe.

He kissed a trail across the curve of one breast, licking before varying his touch with the rougher play of teeth. Her skin tingled, and she stirred restlessly almost purring as he'd threatened.

Please don't stop.

He dragged his tongue around the base of her breast, hard enough to spike sensation and drive her toward pleasure. She melted into the blanket, her limbs loosening, legs parting a fraction in silent encouragement. Her heart knocked against her ribs, the normal slow beat, racing.

Don't stop. Please don't stop.

Leo stopped. "You're tense."

Isabella grabbed him by the ears and forced his mouth toward her breasts. "Don't tease me. Please."

The man chuckled but ceased his dallying. The stubble dusting his jaw brushed her midriff, and the abrasive sensation wrested a rough sigh from her. More. The muscles of her inner thighs quivered while her body softened, moistened, demanded release. It had been so long. Just one touch, one lick across her swollen clit would send her into orbit. She parted her legs even more in a non-subtle hint.

Leo's laugh brought a rush of color to her cheeks. No chills and goose bumps now. Wetness seeped from her pussy while the tickle of heat brought a soft moan.

"Patience, sweetheart. I want to make this good for both of us."

"I don't think delayed gratification is a good thing. Drives people to murder."

Hardly the right time to tell him she'd been waiting for him, wanting him desperately for ages. Dreams had never flared so hot. Thankfully, Mika had boarded the plane, leaving her free to concentrate on Leo. She'd made sure of it. She'd even bribed a stewardess, asking her to check in when the flight arrived in Auckland.

"You're trying to control me again, direct things," he said, a hint of steel buried in the lazy voice.

Oh hell. Don't stop. "I promise I won't say another word, just don't stop. *Please.*" Isabella buttoned her lips.

Leo lifted his head, his eyes sparkling with both humor and desire. Her breath caught, the long denial finding an outlet in clenched hands and tense muscles. She needed him. Wordlessly, she stared back. His pupils dilated with arousal, and they shared an intense look that left her breathless and aching.

"You tear me apart inside. I don't know you, but I want you so bad it hurts." His head lowered and his lips brushed across hers. Softly, so tenderly the touch brought tears to her eyes. No one had shown such caring with her for such a long time. He drew away. "Roll over and come up on your hands and knees."

Isabella stared at him before obeying his order. She rolled and pushed up until she balanced on hands and knees, her heart going even faster than before. From the corner of her eye she caught a movement—Leo grabbing something. The crinkle of foil tearing burst the bubble of tension inside. A sigh of relief whispered past her lips.

He didn't intend to stop.

Seconds later, she sensed him behind her. The touch of his hands at her waist confirmed it. He slipped his hand across her back, callused fingers moving lower to strum across the small green dragon tattoo on the small of her back. A shiver escaped as he repeated the move. She felt the prod of his cock, the slide of his fingers across her backside. She swallowed, nervous.

Then he reached between her legs and parted slick folds with a competent move. Thoughts of his experience flickered to life and faded under his practiced touch. She released the hint of jealousy with her next breath.

One finger drifted across her clit in a teasing pass. Sensation spiraled through her, bringing a gasp. Her stomach muscles contracted, and she bit her bottom lip, waiting for more, for Leo to touch her again.

He grasped her hips with his hands and she savored the bite of fingernails. Her heart lurched when one nail dug deep. She winced but didn't complain, guessing he'd bled into feline. A smile crept to life. Good news because the partial change meant he felt something for her. Whether he knew it or not, she pushed and subtly prodded his feline.

"You okay?" he asked, his voice a low, inaudible growl.

Oh, she could talk now. "Very okay."

"Good."

He widened her stance. A soft breeze blew across her swollen sex. The cool, crisp mountain air along with the scent of dry summer grasses and tussock filled every ragged gasp. Leo's musky arousal danced across her senses. His fingers glided the length of her cleft, the liquid noises embarrassing. She winced but Leo laughed.

"Now," he said, and pushed inside her tight channel with one hard thrust. Fully impaled, he paused, his cock throbbing. He leaned over her, his chest brushing her back and nuzzled

87

the sensitive fleshy skin between neck and shoulder. A guttural curse made her freeze then the nip of teeth dug deeper.

At first, the piercing bite hurt, but pain gave way to pleasure. She shuddered, pulse pounding while the tingle of teeth sent erotic chills skittering across her skin. Leo released his grip on her shoulder. His hips jerked, he sighed, and rasped his tongue across the spot where he'd bitten her. He thrust hard for three strokes, a rough growl vibrating through his chest.

Isabella groaned as pleasure soared, letting Leo do the work and storing up the sensations to savor later. Each stroke drove her higher. He kissed the bite site before scraping his teeth across the spot again. The drag of his teeth pushed into her pain barrier, but each stroke of his cock counteracted with pleasure until she trembled on a knife-edge, her body full of raw yearning, a mass of writhing desire.

Another thrust. Another shimmer of intense pleasure. Thick and throbbing, and oh-so good. Her fingers curled into the blanket, and she pushed back against him. Leo licked her shoulder, the rasp of his tongue rough on her sensitive flesh. Jolts of excitement flowed from random to continuous until she gasped, on the verge of pleading.

"Hurry, Leo. Faster."

Sensing her imminent explosion, he pushed deep, each rapid thrust blurring into the next. A low moan escaped, and climax broke over her in a thunderous wave, the spasms of her vagina clutching his shaft with rhythmic pulses.

Leo groaned, thrust and bit down hard on the fleshy part of her neck, holding on tight while his large frame trembled in orgasm.

Oh god, she thought as another spasm shot through her pussy. She knew what this meant. Tomasine had told her about the birds and the bees—the way of felines. He'd mated her without asking. All she needed to do to complete the bond was reciprocate with a bite of her own. Exhilaration combined with intense fear.

Oh, she loved him. That wasn't an issue, but they couldn't have a future with the past and present holding so many secrets.

Chapter 6

Trouble Stalks Closer

Mika left the flight at Christchurch. Isabella hadn't told him the truth. Why was she in the south of the South Island if her target lived in Auckland? It made little sense, which was why he'd headed back to Queenstown to investigate further. Her long silence also bothered him—unless she wanted to take full credit for the hit and receive the final payment instead of sharing it with him.

But she'd contacted him, told him to come to Queenstown. Mika shook his head, his heart telling him one thing while his head told him something different.

Luckily, he traveled light and leaving the flight earlier posed no problems for him. These days with terrorist plots around every corner, transporting concealed weapons proved difficult, if not impossible. Like any good mercenary, he'd learned to improvise and had a good network of anonymous contacts who provided weapons without questions.

Slinging his black daypack over his right shoulder, Mika strode to the nearest car hire counter. Thirty minutes later, he drove from the airport car park, a plan forming while he negotiated the country roads before hitting the outskirts of Christchurch. He'd do more checking from here, go over last sightings of the target and anything else he could find before returning to Queenstown. He'd had the foresight to plant a tracker beacon in Isabella's handbag. If the woman had started playing games, he'd unravel the problem, and she'd pay.

A mercenary's reputation depended on successful hits, and Mika hated the idea of a blemished record.

L eo had never felt so replete, so satisfied and so bloody confused. He'd bitten her, partially completing the bonding process, even though he didn't know her well.

Fuck, he'd behaved like a Neanderthal.

He hadn't asked. He'd taken.

A glance at the bite site, showed him it still bled and he instinctively lapped away the blood. She wasn't a shifter so how could she understand the urges driving him to claim her, leaving his mark, his scent. His tongue caressed her flesh again. She moaned—a low, hoarse groan—and he froze.

"Hell, I'm sorry. Did I hurt you?" he asked, turning her into his arms so he could read her face.

"What?" She smiled up at him, her eyes at half-mast.

At least she wasn't screaming he was a madman. "I should take you back to the vineyard and grab the first-aid kit."

"No!"

Leo's shoulders slumped, thinking she didn't want to have anything more to do with him. He didn't blame her. He started to stand when she laughed and grabbed him by the shoulders. He toppled, falling on top of her. Before he could apologize again, she grabbed him and clamped their lips together.

He tried to move, but she refused to release him, kissing him again. Interesting. His big, bad alpha act hadn't scared her off. But it'd scared the shit out of him. He resolved to move with caution in the future. She wasn't his mate in the full sense. *Yet.*

She pushed at his shoulder, and still worried about his rough treatment, he rolled away. Isabella moved with speed, straddling his chest, a triumphant smirk on her kissable lips. He blinked up at her. Hell, she'd moved so fast he'd barely had time to formulate a thought. And she was strong. A thought occurred, but after a discreet sniff, he discarded the idea. No way was she a shifter. She smelled the same as every human he'd met, carrying a bouquet of scents—laundry powder, soap, deodorant, shampoo and a natural musk that reminded him of exotic woods and plants.

"Ready for another go-round?"

"Another?" he asked, trying to control his surprise but failing.

"Have I worn you out?"

"Never." Longing sprang to life. His mate. He'd never tire of her, would always want her. He'd known that from the first instant he'd plunged inside her body, felt the connection, her tight channel squeezing his cock.

"That's what I like to hear." Her eyes twinkled with mischief. A good trait for a mate—the ability to tease and banter.

Leo placed his hands under his head to use as a pillow and stared up at her, sure bemusement covered his face. "Now that you have me, what are you intending to do with me?" *Anything she wanted.*

"I figured I'd touch and explore and take things from there."

Leo's body reacted with enthusiasm at the suggestion. With a deep inhalation, he waited for her next move. The sun caught her brown hair, dusting it with fiery red highlights. After the fright she'd given him earlier, she seemed bright and healthy. He'd let her set the pace this time. "Excellent plan."

She laughed, a joyful sound that had a smile tugging at his lips. "I wasn't planning on asking permission."

His brows shot upward. He stirred, testing her hold and couldn't move without a struggle. Before he could comment on her strength, she kissed him again. The swish of her tongue froze him in place while the tight vise of her thighs around his hips held him firmly. He pushed his mind away from the puzzling

93

aspects of her personality. His cock pulsed and thickened, ready for a replay.

"I love a man with a quick recovery time." The mischievous twinkle popped to life again. She nuzzled his neck and licked across the fleshy part between shoulder and neck. It sent an intense shudder through him, the sensation intensifying when she added the scrape of teeth. He willed her to take it further, to bind them together, his breath whooshing out a sigh of disappointment when she moved lower. She quickened her pace, plucking at one flat nipple with thumb and finger. The sharp bite of pain brought both a wince and a surge of lust. Pure, hot need. His pulse lurched to fast and choppy, her touch unraveling him. He waited, tense and on edge, silently pleading. A lick across his collarbone. Another pinch of his nipple.

She moved down his body, maneuvering over his erection, yet still holding him prisoner between her thighs. Not that he wanted to move. The more time he spent with her, the more she intrigued him. A human.

Leo yelped when she pinched him a third time.

"Just making sure you weren't falling asleep."

"Never."

"Good," she said in a severe voice, before removing the sting with the warmth of her mouth. "Because I don't want you to miss this." Her expression turned predatory and she grasped his cock, pumping it within the grip of her hand. She nuzzled his inner thigh, sucking a spot of flesh before grinning up at him.

"You have my full attention." God, he hoped he could keep his feline in line.

Laughing, she lowered her head and lapped across the head of his cock, a delicate lick that tore him apart, pushed at his restraint. Sweet warmth engulfed him as she took his cock into her mouth, and he couldn't prevent the upward strain of his hips, the silent plea for her to take more of him into her wickedly hot mouth.

She did, opening her mouth wider, head bobbing as she took him deeper, tonguing across his crown with exquisite attention to the nerve-rich underside. Meanwhile her fingers stroked the base of his cock and toyed with his tight balls.

Leo swallowed a moan. A fine sheen of sweat popped out on his forehead. He attributed it to the heat of the day until she licked the head of his shaft again. An enormous shudder racked his body, making her laugh. The vibration of her chuckle around his cock felt even better.

"Isabella," he whispered, his hands threading through her hair to hold her in place. If she stopped, he thought he might howl.

She flicked her tongue over the top and down the underside, not too hard, but enough to make him pay attention and wonder what she might do next. She sucked lightly while working the rest of the shaft with her fingers.

A groan slipped free. "Isabella," he whispered. "Yes, perfect."

She laughed again, vibration pulsing through his dick again while the sweep of her tongue, the suction of her mouth drove the sweet pressure higher. He couldn't help the rock of his hips, and when she licked the delicate underside, he thrust.

She didn't seem to mind, but he tried not to frighten her with his surging need. Like a green boy, he shook and trembled, the pleasure rising fast. Then she varied things. Each time he pushed into her mouth, she swallowed, the tightening sensation on his tip exquisite, pushing him, driving him to climax in the most sensual, decadent way. He wondered if she'd swallow or remove the heat of her mouth and watch him shoot. God, that felt good.

Either way, he didn't care. He enjoyed being with Isabella.

"Isabella." The prickle preceding climax flared, and he swallowed audibly. "Isabella, I'm going to come." He tried to move, giving her an option, but her grip tightened and she refused to release him.

Pleasure. Just exquisite pleasure.

Her mouth sucked, taking him deep. She swallowed, squeezing his engorged head, sending a thick slice of enjoyment shooting from his balls and up his shaft. The pressure grew until with a guttural cry, he exploded, dense streams of cum blasting into her mouth.

Slowly he came back to himself, his large hands gently massaging her head.

Their gazes met.

She cleaned his cock and lifted her head to smile. "Ready to eat? I'm starving."

Leo stared, unable to put the fragile emotions into words, his heart still pounding with the force of his release.

Difficult to understand how he could love a woman so soon after meeting her, want to spend the rest of his life with her. His heart knew. His head agreed.

Now all he needed to do was convince her they'd be good together, tell her of his shifter status and get her to complete the mating bond. No sweat.

Letting instinct guide him, Mika hit an internet café to research. He'd booked into an inner-city hotel for the night. First, he checked his email, frowning when he noticed Nelson hadn't checked in. He drummed the fingers of his right hand on the desktop, worry churning his gut. Although they never worked together, they kept in contact. This silence meant one thing.

Nelson was dead.

A Japanese girl in the neighboring booth frowned at him, but Mika ignored her irritation and continued to drum his fingers. Mercenaries who hunted Queen Augustus were dying. He had to face the truth and the inherent danger to him.

The girl huffed her annoyance and his fingers stilled. Mika signed out of his email account and clicked on a search engine. He hesitated while his mind drifted, toying with the problem, the information he knew and the missing parts he had no way of checking.

No matter what way he looked at it, the problem bore two solutions. Either the queen had turned into a skilled killer or she'd met someone to protect her.

No way were the disappearing mercenaries merely good luck for the queen. Mika didn't believe in luck. He believed in skill and planning. It got him through every time.

The computer beeped at him and he fed the meter another two-dollar coin before typing in shifter and clicking the search New Zealand option. Nothing. Although Mika was human through and through, he wasn't stupid enough to ignore stories others wrote off as implausible.

He'd seen Isabella's body spit out a bullet, and that was proof enough for him.

Joseph did amazing shit. He'd witnessed men turning into big cats one day but hadn't been stupid enough to betray his presence and had kept downwind.

Yeah, his human illusions had left him that day. His brows met in a frown and in typed in black cat. Instantly the computer came up with several links. He clicked on the first one.

"Bingo." Elation flowed through him. He minimized the link and called up a map. Middlemarch. Not far from Dunedin and still close to Queenstown. Mika went back and saw a reporter called Tomasine Brooks had written the article. He'd talk to this journalist, ask a few questions. He needed to discover where Isabella lived, and if she continued to hunt, or as he suspected, now worked for Queen Augustus.

Mika's mouth tightened with determination. He needed to finish this hit. He needed the money before his gambling debts became due. Time was a limited commodity.

S aber Mitchell put down the phone, a troubled frown marring his smooth brow.

"What? What's wrong?" Emily placed a mug of coffee in front of him. "Who was on the phone? Was it the h— Ah, the thing?"

Instead of reaching for the coffee, Saber grabbed his wife and drew her onto his knee, wrapping his arms around her waist and nuzzling her hair. He dragged her scent deep into his lungs, allowing the familiar to soothe his unease. "No, as far as I know the thing is underway. We'll hear when it's done."

"You're worried."

"I don't take it lightly, having a man's life ended."

Emily pressed herself against his chest and kissed the bare column of his throat. "Of course you don't. None of us like the idea, but we have proof the man is a monster. He has the local law in his back pocket. We've discussed every alternative. There is no other way."

Saber sighed, knowing she was right. "Yeah, I know. That was the editor of the newspaper Tomasine freelances for. A man called, wanting to discuss the cat story she wrote."

Emily inhaled sharply. "Shit."

"That's one word for it. I told the editor Tomasine is on holiday in Auckland with her new husband and said I'd pass on the message once she returned."

"Tomasine must have given this number as her contact," Emily said. "Do you think we're in danger? Do you think the man is a mercenary?"

"It could be innocent."

"But you don't think so."

"No. My gut tells me we have a problem. There's something else too. Jaime discovered a man's body on his farm earlier today. Shot in the head."

"Anyone we know?"

"No. The police have no idea of his real identity. Turns out the ID he had on him was false."

Emily nodded, her hands clutching his biceps. Saber didn't protest. The same tension resided in his gut. He'd do anything to keep his family safe. *Anything*. He'd always been responsible for his brothers. His mating with Emily had given him even more responsibilities. *Those* were a pleasure. He loved Emily with every particle of his body. He'd have to send her away.

Emily tipped up her head and stared him straight in the eye. "Don't send me away, Saber Mitchell, not if you know what's good for you."

His gut tightened, the predator in him sensing the coming fight. "I can't concentrate on what needs to be done if I'm worried."

Emily cupped his face with one hand, the gentle touch arcing straight to his groin despite his worry. God, he loved this woman. If something happened to her…

"I need to be part of this, Saber. I can't leave and sit around wondering what's happening. Why don't you contact Leo and ask him to come home? Some of your feline friends would help. All you need to do is ask. Besides, we don't know for sure a mercenary is coming. This dead man might not be connected."

Saber's gut twisted, his love for Emily bringing both pleasure and pain. In truth, he'd hate her leaving. He loathed sleeping alone. Maybe she was right. Coming to a decision, he kissed her, taking his own sweet time. He took tiny bites of her lips, and when she opened her mouth to him, he let his tongue slide inside to mate with hers. When they pulled apart, Emily looked dazed and he couldn't help a smug, satisfied grin. He lifted her and set her on her feet before standing to reach for the phone. Seconds later, he was talking to Leo.

"Leo, can you come home?"

"Problem?" Leo's casual voice turned sharp, packing questions into the single word.

"Possibly." Saber heard a feminine voice in the background and bit back amusement. Leo attracted women like a fresh cowpat attracted flies on a summer day.

"Okay if I leave early tomorrow morning?"

Saber knew he could count on the other members of the council and neighbors if he needed help tonight. "Yeah, that'll work. I thought I might invite Saul to stay. We could do with help on the farm. Emily was saying we haven't seen him for a good month."

"I'll come now," Leo said.

"No, tomorrow's okay. I'm overreacting." But he didn't think so. His stomach lurched with renewed anxiety. If it had been an inquiry regarding the black cats, his alarm bells wouldn't have screeched, but the person had wanted to talk to Tomasine—the part that alarmed him. And there was the dead stranger.

"See you tomorrow then," Leo said.

"Make sure you get sleep," Saber said with a wink at Emily.

"Yeah. No worries." Leo disconnected, wiping the smirk from Saber's face.

"Another problem?" Emily asked.

"Leo had a woman with him."

"That's a problem?"

"He didn't make a joke when I told him to get some sleep."

"Maybe he's worried about events here."

"Nah, I think he's found her."

Emily moved into his arms and dragged down his head. "Your instincts are working overtime, Mr. Mitchell. I can distract you as soon as you've contacted your friends."

The wave of love for his mate threatened to buckle his knees. Instead, he swallowed the lump from his throat and reached for the phone again. While the call was going through, he smiled at Emily. "We have the house to ourselves for once. We should take advantage of the privacy."

"Damn straight," she said, her grin saucy and suggestive. "Meet you in the bedroom."

Chapter 7

Sweet Seduction

"I s there a problem?" Isabella asked. They'd traveled back to Queenstown late afternoon and hustled straight to Leo's room to pick up where they'd left off. The cotton sheets rustled as she wriggled to a more comfortable position.

Leo climbed off the bed and strode to the window. He stared out before turning to her. "Nothing important, although I need to return to Middlemarch early tomorrow morning instead of spending the entire day here."

Isabella frowned, frustrated because she couldn't say anything to him, not with secrets between them still. She'd heard both sides of the conversation thanks to her acute shifter hearing. Saber had said little. Enough to alarm her though. What had happened to make Saber call the family together? He hadn't mentioned Tomasine and Felix, which implied they were safe.

She tried to tamp down her frustration. The calmness that was so easy and a part of her makeup failed her.

Leo's fault.

The feline had marked her, claimed her as his but hadn't uttered a word afterward. He'd left her dangling and she couldn't reciprocate with the mark because Leo might suspect her knowledge of shifters and ask questions. Now trouble was brewing in Middlemarch. She fought the frown pulling at her mouth to hide her concern.

Leo stalked the perimeter of the room.

"That's too bad," she murmured, watching the muscles flex in Leo's arse as he paced past her. The view looked mighty fine from both directions. Hard to pick her favorite panorama. Isabella shook away the distracted thoughts to concentrate. He was leaving. Their little idyll was over. "I'll miss you."

Leo stopped mid-pace and whirled to fix her with an intense look. "You could come with me."

Although her initial instinct was to shout *yes*, she couldn't go to Middlemarch with Leo. Not yet. She had to check on Mika and make sure he'd deplaned in Auckland. And if he returned, she'd stop him from finding Tomasine. "I can't. I have another job interview set up for Monday morning."

"Can you change the time?"

"No." Her throat tightened with regret, and not for the first time the weight of lies constricted her mind. "There's a lot of competition for the spots. I won't get another chance. But you're not leaving until tomorrow morning, right?" Isabella dropped the sheet to reveal her naked breasts and held out her arms. "We have the rest of the evening and tonight."

Leo sent her a hard, searching look. It appeared as if he'd say something, but he shrugged, a slow, sexy smile blooming. It made his green eyes glow, made her feel ultrafeminine and attractive, something she hadn't felt for a long time. Tension seeped into her lower belly, the caress of his eyes stealing her breath. *Oh my.*

His gaze flicked to her shoulder and lingered on the spot where he'd marked her earlier. Heat suffused her, radiating from the mark, sweeping across her shoulders, plumping her breasts and coalescing at her clit. Words trembled on her lips, a demand for Leo to rasp his tongue over the raised wound, to make her burn.

The plea remained unuttered. Wedged between a rock of truth and her fabrications. Isabella shuddered, and it wasn't all heat and arousal. For the first time fear stalked her mind, anxiety that she'd fail and lose everything. She snorted at the fanciful thoughts—failure wasn't an option—and concentrated on the man instead. Tomorrow was soon enough to face her doubts.

Tonight was about sex, about pleasure. Tonight was about love.

"Touch me," she demanded, leaning back against the plump pillows.

"Where?" His lazy grin ratcheted up her awareness, chased away concern and uncertainties, replacing it with pure, hot desire. "Where should I touch you?"

Isabella shrugged, her breasts lifting with shift of her shoulders. His watchful eyes scanned her and the visual caress was almost physical. "Anywhere. Everywhere."

"I'd rather you showed me what turns you on."

"Show you?" Masturbate in front of him? Her eyes narrowed, wondering what he wanted from her. "Why?"

"Scared?"

"Never."

"Show me then." Leo sat on the bed beside her and took her hand, lacing their fingers together. "I believe in some countries a woman's neck is considered sexy." He trailed their linked fingers across the base of her throat, ending close to the mark. A pulse leaped to life just below her jaw and her heart echoed the flutter. Moisture gathered at the entrance to her pussy and her channel clenched. One short, sharp demand for Leo. She needed him to fill her, to fuck her and ease the ache inside. His fingers flexed, bumping the outer edge of the bite site.

Please touch it, she thought. *Please*.

But instead, he directed their joined hands on a different path. They brushed across the upper slopes of her breasts, back and forth until her skin tingled and she felt heavy and warm. The contrast in their skin colors, his much darker than her own, sent a jolt of desire sizzling up and down her spine.

"There," he whispered, watching her lips. "That wasn't so bad. Now you show me."

Isabella frowned, still uneasy despite knowing he'd never hurt her. Showing vulnerability in front of him—it went against her nature, every particle of self-protection. But this was Leo. A Mitchell and the man she loved...

He traced the furrow between her brows with a forefinger until it smoothed away. "You don't have to if I scare you that much."

"You don't scare me."

"No?"

"No." Isabella strove for firmness. Confidence. "Make yourself comfortable, and I'll show you." Vulnerability jumped to the fore, but she could bluff her way through. She'd show him.

Leo plumped two pillows and arranged them against the wooden headboard. He sprawled back, comfortable and at ease with his nakedness.

After a deep breath, Isabella commenced. She wanted to keep her eyes open but they drifted shut, and when he didn't comment, she left them that way because it was easier with her vision screened. She trailed her fingers across her collarbone, accidentally touching the raised edge of the mark. Her heart hammered, a frisson of pleasure taking her unaware. Her pussy rippled again, the emptiness almost painful. She needed cock. Leo's to be precise.

"Don't stop." His warm breath wafting over her earlobe, stirring a reaction that skittered to her pelvis. "Carry on. You've barely started."

"I'm...I'm not stopping. You've heard about expectation? Anticipation?"

He chuckled, the husky sound raising a ripple of goose bumps across her arms and legs. "There's also cowardice." The words were a taunt she couldn't ignore.

"Watch this, smartass." Good thing she couldn't see his face because her heart thundered in excitement while her stomach muscles drew tight. She stuck her right forefinger into her mouth and wet it with saliva. Then she drew patterns across her left breast, arching her back when her finger drew closer and closer to her puckered nipple.

Her skin prickled, the pleasure and pattern of the lazy touches shooting arousal to her clit. With each touch, her pussy ached for him. She went to lick her digit again but he grabbed her hand.

"Let me." An instant later, his lips, warm and wet, closed around the tip. He strummed his tongue back and forth across the tip and sucked. Isabella moaned, feeling the tug of his mouth all the way to her sex. Finally, he pulled back. "Carry on," he said, shifting his weight and his position. The mattress gave, jostling their bodies together from hip to knee. "Go on. I'm enjoying this."

Her lashes fluttered open to his intent look, the indolent grin. Without breaking their connection, she slipped her damp finger down the slope of her breast and circled the pink areola. The moist path she left prickled with sensitivity. Her nipple pulled tight and Isabella tugged hard enough to send a nip of pain through her. Suddenly caressing her breast wasn't enough. The ache in her pussy had grown and she needed more. Swallowing, she eased her legs apart and slipped her hand across her rib cage, over her hip. She hesitated, feeling his interest.

"Go on," he urged. "Show me so I can duplicate it another time."

"You know enough about giving a woman pleasure," Isabella said tartly, her green-eyed monster leaping to the fore at the thought of the other women—even though her resentment wasn't fair or smart. "You don't need me to show you."

"Anyone would think you were jealous of the women in my past."

"Maybe." The truth escaped, and she bit her lip to stop any more confidences escaping. Heck, oversharing.

A gentle smile highlighted the arousal in his expression—a smile that turned sinful as he shifted his position so he faced her. "You have no need. I'm with you now."

Isabella closed her eyes and pain struck. For how long?

"True," she whispered, pushing the words past the lump in her throat. "So I'll show you. Pay attention because I'll only do this once."

"I'm watching. I can see the petal lips, the moisture weeping from your pretty sex, and your swollen clit, peeping out from under its hood. And smell your arousal. It's making me ravenous," he said in a husky growl.

She trembled as urgency slammed her, punching the air from her lungs like the force of a blow. Her eyes flickered open. God help her but she needed him, wanted him to pound into her pussy, taking and possessing her until pleasure claimed them both. A shiver whispered across her skin while they stared at each other, sensual tension palpable.

"Go on," he whispered, his dark voice full of encouragement. Hunger.

Isabella battled the fear stalking her mind and won, for the moment, but her hand shook as she lifted it to her mouth to moisten her finger for a second time. She began the process over again, circling her breast, stroking the underside and coming closer and closer to her nipple. She pinched it between finger and thumb. The small pain flew across her nerve endings and her vagina pulsed in hunger.

A sharp gasp escaped. She desperately wanted to stop, but equally craved an ending to assuage the sharp need that threatened to consume her.

While the fingers of one hand continued to tease and taunt her nipple, her other hand smoothed over her rib cage and her stomach. The nerves jumped beneath her skin and she could smell her own arousal, the honey seeping from her entrance. Her legs quaked when she widened her stance, the unnerving weight of Leo's stare prodding both nerves and arousal to sharp life.

Isabella skated her fingers across the top of her thigh, bypassing her slit. But even though she kept her touch confined, demand spiraled upward, turning her entire body into one big erogenous zone.

"Do it, Isabella. Smooth your juices over your clit. Pump a finger into your pussy and come for me."

Heat suffused her body in one big wave, a flush of heat rushing across her face and chest. Isabella swallowed her lingering doubts and obeyed. She brushed her finger along her cleft, gathering the honey that had gathered at her entrance. She smoothed it over her swollen clit, using delicate touches with a slight rotation. Almost instantly, she felt the prickle of climax. Too soon. *Too soon*. She gentled the touch, tamping down until she knew she could control it, make it last.

"Would you like me to help?"

"Yes. I need...I want...please." She couldn't watch, couldn't look at him, not right now with her emotions in turmoil. Her lashes swept low, blotting out everything except the sensations threatening to annihilate her.

The mattress depressed when Leo moved closer then she felt him. A heated but delicate touch.

"I love your taste. Delicious." His hands forced her thighs farther apart and he nipped her inner thigh. Then his tongue—a long, slow-rasping lick.

"Leo."

"Keep that finger moving. If you stop, I'll stop too. You wouldn't want that."

No, she never wanted him to stop.

He licked around her finger, giving a delicate lick before he prodded her entrance. The roughness of his tongue produced a flutter of excitement and an intense rush that foretold orgasm. With a languorous rub, she pushed herself toward the cliff and arched upward.

Her pussy pulsed, but despite his attentions, she still felt empty.

"Your finger inside me," she said, biting off a moan at the increasing pleasure. "*Please.*"

"I can do better than that." And he moved over her, guiding his shaft to her entrance, filling her in one hard plunge. Once embedded, he stilled and she pulsed around his shaft. "Carry on," he said. "This is your show."

Isabella gasped. She ground her hips, attempting to entice him to thrust, to give her more, but he held himself still, watchful. "But you have to thrust."

"No, you were showing me what you want and need to come."

"But you won't get anything in return," she snapped.

"Yes," he said. "I will."

The stupid, stubborn man. He wouldn't change his mind—experience had shown his determination. Her lips curled back in a snarl, she gritted her teeth. Her finger caressed and fondled. A little direct stimulation before backing off. If he wouldn't help her, she'd make him suffer.

Isabella became wetter, her breasts so tight and needy they ached. She squeezed one nipple while rubbing her clit. The spasms of her vagina came faster, hard, and Leo's cock grew longer, a firm, hard warmth inside, something for her to flex against.

"That's it, sweetheart." He whispered encouragement, his voice rougher.

The prickle of climax built higher. She groaned and stroked faster, the hand at her breast tightening and pushing into pain. The tension ramped up and her head fell back, soft cries escaping. Her finger stroked one final time and suddenly she was flying, her pussy clamping hard on Leo's cock, pleasure scalding her. Her back bowed and she let go of her nipple to grip Leo's shoulders. Their mouths met and he moved, hard strokes that pounded into her fevered flesh. Her channel clenched with fresh hunger and a second orgasm, less intense, tore through her.

Sounds of fucking thickened the pleasure as he invaded her body. Slammed into her. Once. Twice. He groaned as semen spurted in hot blasts, as he drove into her until the contractions faded.

Isabella gripped him tight, sighing against his shoulder and drawing his scent deep into her lungs. Even if she hadn't loved him, he'd spoiled her for other men.

No one would do except Leo.

Nothing like ratcheting up the pressure and stress. Somehow, she had to juggle the balls she had in play, and do it well, because failure wasn't an option, not if she wanted a future with him.

Chapter 8

Worries Circle

Leo drove to Middlemarch on autopilot, his mind circling worries of the situation at home and sheer panic at the thought of losing Isabella. Even after spending a full day and night with her, Leo had no idea of where he stood. Yeah, the sex was great, but she'd held back.

He tapped his fingers on the steering wheel. Hell, he couldn't believe he'd marked her.

If she walked away, he'd remain tied to her.

Fool. If he'd misjudged her in the heat of the moment because his heart craved his mate...fuck, just call him a eunuch. Stupid romantic fool fit the situation better. Leo thumped the steering wheel with his left hand and cursed. Hell, what a fuckin' mess. His brothers would kill themselves laughing.

When they'd parted, Isabella had smiled and kissed him, but had given no indication of her feelings. The woman had enigmatic down pat.

"Can I see you again?" he'd asked.

"Sure, look me up next time you're in Queenstown." An offhand, casual reply that set warning signals flaring inside. Had she slept with him because he was a challenge? A pretty face to collect and discard?

In desperation, he'd grabbed one of his business cards from the vineyard and scrawled his home number on the back. Leo's chest ached and his throat felt so damn tight his repeated swallowing didn't ease the tension. He'd screwed up.

Secrets. They shimmered between them, so tangible he could almost touch them. He remembered the brief flicker of her sexy eyes, so swift most people wouldn't have noticed. Yeah, secrets. Instinct told him she had them and they'd stop her from contacting him.

A black motorbike passed him during the midpoint of his journey and a carload of teenagers overtook with a screech of wheels when he reached the outskirts of Middlemarch. The roads were quiet, even for a Sunday morning. Fifteen minutes later, he pulled up outside the Mitchell homestead. Things were quiet inside, but he didn't panic since he could hear Saber and Emily's soft murmurs. Leo headed for the kitchen and started the coffeemaker. No doubt, his brother and sister-in-law had heard him arrive home.

Leo had poured his first cup by the time Saber prowled into the room. He stood, grabbed two more cups from the cupboard, filled them with coffee and set them on table.

"Morning, Leo." Emily breezed in and grabbed the seat next to Saber, scooting closer so she could cuddle. The fresh scent of citrus shampoo and soap drifted to him. Both had damp hair, indicating a recent shower, and they glowed with happiness.

Normally Leo would have teased them, but today he experienced the lack in his own life. Hell, what was he going to do about Isabella? It was too early to say he loved her. He knew that, but he couldn't imagine being with another woman. He didn't want another woman. "Morning."

Emily pulled away from Saber and cocked her head to the side. "You look tired." Her attention zeroed in on his neck, and her eyes crinkled with delight. "Hickey. Did you have a busy weekend?"

Leo snorted. "Saber should paddle your backside more often."

"You leave Emily's backside out of this discussion," Saber said. "I have everything under control."

"That's what he thinks," Emily said, her grin plain impish.

Leo couldn't help returning her smile and wondered how Isabella would get on with Emily and Tomasine, his brothers. Didn't look as if he'd find out.

"What's wrong?" Emily asked.

"I don't want to discuss it. What's going on here?"

"Someone rang the newspaper in Dunedin asking for contact details for Tomasine," Saber said. "It might mean nothing, but the inquiry didn't feel right. The guy wouldn't leave his name or a phone number, which made me suspicious. And there's

117

another mystery body. Jamie found him on his farm. Last I heard they hadn't discovered his true identity. He was using ID for someone who died years ago in London."

"Hell. No one heard anything? Was he shot like the guy we found when Sylvie went missing?"

"Gunshot to the head," Saber said.

"I didn't ask how the man died. Do you think it was a hit?" Emily asked.

Saber shrugged. "I'm not sure what to think."

Leo took a sip of his coffee. "If it was a genuine query, the guy would leave contact details." If Isabella felt genuine emotion for him, she'd have given him a phone number. He blinked. Slowly. Time to concentrate on Mitchell problems. "Do we know anything else?"

"No," Emily said. "We'll have to watch and wait, which means we can discuss your problems."

Leo resisted the urge to fidget when Saber turned his attention on him as well. "I don't have any."

"The tips of your ears are turning pink. When are you and your brothers going to learn you can't lie to me? All I have to do is look at your ears."

Leo set his coffee down before concentrating on Saber.

"Don't look at me. Why do you think I've grown my hair?"

Emily slapped Saber on the arm. "If I find out you've lied about stuff, you're in trouble."

"I met my mate," Leo said. "I marked her."

"You— Where is she?" Saber exchanged a speaking glance with Emily.

Easy to interpret—puzzlement. "I asked her to come home with me. She refused."

"Why?" Emily demanded, looking upset on his behalf. "What's wrong with the woman?"

Leo picked up his coffee cup and put it back on the table because his hand trembled. Fuck, he was falling apart. He swallowed before attempting to speak. "Don't blame Isabella. It wasn't her fault. I was so certain she was my mate, I rushed things." His shoulders moved in a shrug. "Just my usual impulsive self."

Saber ignored his confession despite the number of lectures over the years about first considering situations from all angles. "Did you explain the significance of the bite to Isabella?"

"No." Discussing his actions now made them seem stupid and juvenile. Shallow even. He had a brain beneath the pretty packaging, but no shifter listening to this conversation would believe it.

Emily's dark brows rose. "Didn't she say something when you bit her? Make a comment? Say, 'Fuck, that hurt. What the hell are you snacking on me for?' Surely she asked questions?"

"No. We were...ah...busy," Leo said.

"Is she a shifter?" asked Saber. "That might explain her lack of questions."

Emily shook her head in vehement disagreement. "I'd ask questions. I *do* ask questions."

SHELLEY MUNRO

"She's not a shifter," Leo said. "One-hundred-percent human. She's from Switzerland, over in New Zealand on a working holiday."

"Call her again," Saber said. "Invite her to stay and dangle a job at the vineyard as bait."

"She works in hotels, which was the reason she gave for staying. She has an interview tomorrow and didn't want to miss it."

"Maybe she's one of those who enjoy pain." Emily fixed a curious gaze on him, eyes full of speculation. "Did you—?"

Thankfully, Saber clapped his fingers over Emily's mouth and halted the inevitable stream of questions. "That's enough, sweetheart. You don't like my brothers asking about our sex life." He moved his hand with a sudden yelp.

"But they listen and comment," she said tartly. "Oh, don't be such a big baby. I didn't bite hard."

"We don't listen on purpose, Emily," Leo said. "We try to give you privacy."

"Did you at least get a contact phone number?" Emily asked.

"Short answer. No. I tried. What do I do now?"

"Go back to Queenstown and wear her down. Mitchell men are notoriously stubborn," Emily said with a sniff in Saber's direction. "Some might call it bossy."

"I can't go now. I'm needed here," Leo said, trying to ignore the pangs of anxiety in his chest. He couldn't lose Isabella, not now that he'd found her. Somehow, he'd woo her and they'd complete the marking. He refused to settle for less. "What's the plan?"

Saber frowned. "We're closing ranks and watching for strangers who ask too many questions. That's all we can do at the moment."

"At least we know Felix and Tomasine are safe." Emily scowled. "And Gina? Won't she be in danger with us?"

"But one of us would have to take her to the farm," Leo said. "We can't risk anyone following."

"We'd better get her to come home," Saber said. "Leo, you will have to watch her for us. Don't let her out of your sight. She likes you and won't think of you as a jailer."

"Yeah, okay." Leo dragged his hand through his hair, impatient to woo Isabella but his family came first right now. "But I warn you, if she starts giggling, I'm handing her back to you, Emily. That giggle grates like fingernails on a chalkboard."

Emily glanced at clock and jumped to her feet. "I've got to go to the café. Leo, I'll take half shifts with you. Gina likes cooking. I can set her to work in the kitchen and keep her out of trouble. Saber, the number for the Robertsons is by the phone. Can you ring them and one of you pick up Gina? Leo, bring her to Storm in a Teacup this afternoon." Instructions issued, she raced off, leaving both brothers staring after her.

Finally, Leo shook his head, listening to the sound of the car as Emily left. "And she thinks we're bossy."

Saber grinned. "Great, isn't she?"

In the past, Leo might have teased his brother, but today he didn't have it in him. Saber's grin faded and he morphed back into the head of the family—strong and powerful. Authoritative.

"You should be able to find Isabella easily enough now that you've marked her. I can sense Emily is nearby even if I can't see her. She says she can do the same thing despite being human."

The tension in Leo eased a fraction. He'd worried about finding Isabella. "What if she leaves Queenstown?"

"Don't worry. We'll find her." Saber stood to grab the phone and the number for the Robertsons.

Leo topped up his coffee and filled Saber's, handing it over to his brother. He slumped into his chair and moodily recalled the last two days. He didn't think he'd do much different. Isabella was his mate. She might think she'd keep her secrets, but along with his impulsiveness, he had Mitchell stamina and determination plus the knowledge his family was on his side. He had the advantage even if it didn't feel like it.

"She what?" Saber's voice boomed through the kitchen, jerking Leo from his problems. "She hasn't been there at all? Could I speak to your daughter?" Saber paused to listen then apologized. "I'm sorry, I didn't mean to shout. We understood Gina was spending the weekend with you. I see. Does your daughter have any idea where she is? Okay. Yes, I'll ring when I hear something." Saber replaced the phone. "Gina isn't there. They haven't seen her this weekend, and the daughter isn't talking."

"When did you expect her home?" Gina's crush might make him uncomfortable but he liked the kid. She was family. "Do you think someone's snatched her, or is she sneaking around being a teenager?"

"Either way we have trouble." Saber checked his watch and grabbed his car keys. "We can shift the cattle in the top paddock later this afternoon. I'm off to the café. You coming?"

Isabella hadn't expected the weekend to end with so much left unsaid. When Leo had asked for a contact number, she'd panicked. Her. The calm and cool assassin who held control in her palm, forming it into whatever shape she desired. A snort escaped. Except for the last few days when calm had jumped out the window.

Isabella paced the tiled floor of her kitchen, knowing she'd have to stop stressing and do some solid planning. Besides, the kitchen lacked room for proper pacing.

Business. She yanked out a plain wooden chair and slumped into it. *Concentrate*. Sighing, she reached for the backpack where she'd crammed her handbag and a prepaid cell phone, her Gina cell, along with a change of clothes for window dressing. As usual, the phone had disappeared into the twilight zone at the bottom of her handbag.

With a grunt of displeasure, she upended the handbag, strewing the contents over the brown top of the breakfast bar that doubled as a table. Something small and silver bounced off the counter and hit the white tiled floor. Isabella froze, a slither of fear holding her in place for a dazed second. Then she scrambled to grab it. An instant later, she held the silver tracker between her finger and thumb.

"Fuck."

Trouble. Of the Mika sort. If she discounted Leo, Mika was the sole person who'd come close enough to plant the tracking device. Isabella stood and crushed the bug beneath the heel of her black boot. She grabbed her phone and dialed the contact she'd organized to make sure Mika deplaned in Auckland.

With a troubled frown, she hung up minutes later. Bad news. Mika had left the flight during the brief stopover in Christchurch, which meant trouble. Something she'd done had set off his inner alarm. And instinct told her the trouble Saber had alluded to during the phone call with his brother concerned Mika.

This was her fault.

She'd practically drawn a map for Mika. He'd hang around and wait until everyone thought it was safe for Felix and Tomasine to return home. They wouldn't know what hit them. Anxiety stabbed her chest. She rubbed her breastbone and struggled to force air past the band constricting her lungs.

She had to fix this. *Now*.

Her pink Gina cell picked that moment to trill out a latest hit. She'd allocated this song to her friend. Shit, only one reason for Suzie Robertson to ring at this time of the day.

Busted. This day just kept getting better and better.

Isabella morphed to her Gina form, plugged in her password, and answered the phone in persona. Although she didn't need to do this, it helped her concentrate and keep the character traits constant.

"Gina, I'm sorry. My mother told Mr. Mitchell you haven't been with me all weekend."

And she could just imagine Saber's reaction to that confidence. No doubt about it. Gina was hip deep in trouble and grounded. "It's okay."

"Mum said Mr. Mitchell went quiet and polite after his initial shouting."

Isabella wrinkled her nose. *Great. Just great.* "Was it Saber?" It sure sounded like Saber. Suzie knew about her crush on Leo, and since they referred to him by his Christian name, she figured the mister related to Saber.

"I think so. Will they punish you?"

"Yeah. Don't worry. I'll ring you once I get home." Isabella ended the call and morphed back to her previous form. She'd have to return to Middlemarch and front up to face Saber's wrath.

Oh, joy.

Immediate problems first. *Mika*. Isabella wandered the interior of the cottage. She did a circle past the drop cloths covering the furniture in the lounge, hurtled along the hall and turned into her bedroom before repeating the travel path in reverse. What to do? What to do?

125

One alternative. Mika was on his way to Middlemarch. She might as well confirm her presence here and tell him she'd found a lead. The trick would be taking him out without alerting the Mitchells or endangering any of the residents or herself.

Isabella sucked in a deep breath, her fists clenching. She'd do it. She'd managed so far without hurting any innocents. Hopefully, this would be the last time, since once the hit went down on Joseph in Africa, the one on Tomasine ended.

An hour later, after leaving a voice mail for Mika and formulating her plan, Isabella locked her cottage and left for Middlemarch. Aware Leo was there, she shifted into a skinny dark-skinned male with long, greasy hair and lots of dark stubble. Leo wouldn't recognize her in this guise.

Isabella straddled the bike and started up, riding the bike to her usual storage place in Middlemarch. Without drawing attention to herself, she morphed her leathers to T-shirt and faded and ripped black jeans before swaggering along the road to Storm in a Teacup. Best she scope out the café first.

When she saw Emily, she'd get a sense of how worried they were and how much trouble she was in. She pushed through the door, the doorbell ringing chirpily and announcing her arrival.

Emily appeared from the kitchen out the back and gave her a practiced smile. "Good afternoon."

"Hello," Isabella drawled in her masculine voice. "Quiche, salad and flat white." She wanted to snicker because real men didn't eat quiche according to a magazine article she'd read, but remained true to her disguise and handed over a twenty-dollar note. Emily never blinked but handed over change and told her she'd bring the meal in a few minutes. She didn't seem worried or upset.

Interesting. Saber hadn't told her yet.

An elderly couple occupied one table while out in the garden a noisy family held court, their dog running about with two small boys. The joyous barking and laughter of the children brought a smile to Isabella. A pang of envy followed. She'd never had a childhood like that, not with two assassin parents. Her juvenile years had comprised careful training for the future so she could work alongside her parents.

No options. No alternatives. Not a trace of affection or love.

Was it any wonder she'd shifted allegiance? Tomasine had saved a stranger at the risk of her own life. The woman had sheltered and shielded Isabella ever since. As far as Isabella was concerned, Tomasine was an angel and she'd exchange her life in repayment for the affection she'd showered on her.

Second to Tomasine came the rest of the Mitchell clan. They'd accepted her without hesitation, and Isabella would never forget the debt she owed them. Unknowingly, they'd saved her from a life of death and darkness.

She took a seat by the window in order to watch the comings and goings. Her contact hadn't been able to trace Mika's whereabouts, but she had to assume he'd either caught a flight back to Queenstown or had hired a car in Christchurch. If he'd taken the car option, he'd take a day or two to drive to Middlemarch, which gave her time to prepare.

Emily arrived with her meal and set it on the table. "Traveling through?" she asked.

"On my way to Queenstown," Isabella said.

"Looks as if the weather will be good for you." Emily nodded, offered another friendly smile, and headed for the counter where she started making Isabella's coffee.

The whir of the grinder blasted through the quiet café. Comfortable, familiar sounds. Gina spent happy hours in the café helping Emily. At first, it had been to keep a close eye on the visitors coming through Middlemarch, but soon she enjoyed cooking and Emily's irrepressible humor.

The doorbell jingled, indicating another arrival. Isabella's spine snapped upright until it hit the back of her chrome chair. He prowled from the door to the counter, his face an impenetrable mask. Isabella caught Emily's welcoming smile, saw it fade to distinct worry. Saber disappeared into the kitchen while Emily made Isabella's coffee. She delivered it to Isabella, the faint tremor of her hand making the cup rattle once in the saucer.

"Can I get you anything else?"

"I'm good," Isabella answered, her heart knocking against her ribs. Guilt at worrying Saber made her bite her bottom lip. The small pain jerked her back to reality. Lip biting didn't fit the current character. Abruptly she smoothed out her face and jumped back into the male psyche. "Thanks."

Emily hurried away to join Saber in the kitchen. Isabella eavesdropped on the conversation, glad for once that extra-good hearing was part of the chameleon package.

"Gina is missing. She didn't spend the weekend with the Robertsons," Saber said.

"But... I didn't check with Suzie's mother because the girls spend so many weekends together. Do you think something has happened?"

"I'm hoping Gina has snuck off to meet a boy," Saber gritted out. "But that's bad enough."

"What if she gets pregnant or catches a disease?" Emily asked, horror tingeing her voice. "Tomasine and Felix won't speak to me." She sounded close to tears.

"What did she say to you?"

"She offered to help me and mentioned she wanted to spend time with her friends before school starts. I told her to go ahead because she helps so much already. She mentioned Suzie, and I assumed she'd be with them." Emily inhaled with a harsh sound. "The wretch. She won't fool me again."

"When is she due back?"

"This afternoon. Where could she be, Saber?"

"Sweetheart, don't cry. It sounds as if she's stretching her wings."

"But what if she doesn't return?"

"We'll find her, and when we do, she'd better have a good explanation," he finished in an implacable voice.

"Damn straight," Emily added. "She's going to be doing so many dishes her hands will never be the same."

Despite the sense of her past and future running on a collision course, Isabella couldn't prevent the quirk of her lips. During her years as a mercenary, she'd had lots of threats leveled at her. Emily's death by dishpan hands was a new one.

Chapter 9

Unsettled

Once Saber left to meet with Emily, Leo drove out to the old woolshed paddock. He parked his vehicle and climbed out. It wasn't where he wanted to be. Queenstown and Isabella beckoned. Sighing, Leo leaped over the fence and strode up the long slope to the top paddock. Angst burrowed deep, curling through his mind and body. Normally he would have shifted and gone for a long run. Not today.

He reached the gate in record time and opened it to let the cattle drift into the lower paddock at their leisure. Half an hour later, he was back at the homestead.

"Gina!" he shouted.

Silence mocked him. Damn, as much as she irritated and made him uncomfortable, he wanted her safe. He jogged to the phone to call the café, hanging up again after a few terse words with Saber.

No one had asked more questions about Tomasine and no sign of Gina. Yet. They were hoping she'd be back this afternoon as stated. Leo wouldn't like to be in her shoes, and meanwhile, he had to hang around waiting for her.

Leo grabbed a copy of the *Otago Daily Times* and dropped into a scruffy armchair. Emily wanted to replace the furniture, but so far the Mitchell brothers had stood unified. They liked the comfortable chairs they'd had for years and didn't want to break in new ones. He knew they'd lose. Eventually Emily would have her way because as she said, change was good.

His days of being single had ended the minute he'd marked Isabella. *Change.* His snort echoed in the silent room. For once, his pretty face hadn't brought him what he wanted. Isabella had let him leave.

The sports section dropped to the floor while he let his thoughts drift. His eyes grew heavy and he fell asleep with his mind on Isabella and morning sex...

Their bodies brushed together in the shower while warm water pummeled them from several different angles. He cupped her face and stole a kiss, laughing when she grabbed his arse and squeezed. A thick slice of pleasure speared straight to his groin and when she let her hands slide around to tease his balls, he had to have her. *Again.*

With just a few judicious touches, his dick strained up toward his stomach and he rocked his pelvis forward. But guilt nudged at him. She had to be sore after the afternoon and night. He didn't want to force himself on her and cause pain.

"I won't break," she scoffed, reading his mind with ease.

Leo wondered if he should worry, but she grasped his shoulders and levered herself up, her legs curling around his waist and focusing his attention elsewhere. The heat of her pussy seared his thick cock, her glistening folds telling him she wanted him as badly as he wanted her. They slid together with exquisite friction, such perfect synchronicity.

"Fill me," she whispered, guiding his cock to her entrance as she uttered the words. Isabella sank downward and nibbled along his collarbone toward his neck. Her teeth sank into the fleshy part at the base of shoulder and neck, the exact place he'd bitten her.

Leo froze for an instant, willing her to bite harder, willing it to happen, for them to become mates in all ways. His shaft swelled, fire and chills warring within his body and he bit back a cry of disappointment when she released his skin to brush a kiss across his lips. He rocked his pelvis forward, lifted her and let her sink back down, taking him into her tight pussy. Moving faster and faster, she snapped her hips, internal muscles flexing and rippling around his shaft. The electric feel of orgasm raced through him.

"Isabella." He gripped and with a hoarsely voiced curse, he came in explosive contractions. For a moment, he luxuriated in the aftershocks before he kissed her and slipped a finger between their bodies. It didn't take much, just a light massage of her slippery clit and she gave a cry of surrender, slumping against his chest while the water still poured over them.

The trill of the phone broke into his dream and he jerked awake, swore, wiped his palm across his face. Somehow, he had to convince Isabella they were meant for each other and tell her about the mark.

He wanted to wear it with pride.

He craved Isabella's mark.

Isabella left the café after she'd eaten her meal. Uneasy at the worry she was causing, she decided to return, although she still didn't know what story she'd tell. Better think of something quick.

After a glance each way, she ducked behind a pine tree and transformed into Gina. With distaste, she glanced at her tight jeans and brief T-shirt. The outfit did nothing for her figure, highlighting every teenage roll of fat. Sure, her plain looks kept away the boys. Who wanted the aggravation of hormone-crazy teen boys chasing after her? But she didn't feel sexy or feminine, and for once, that stuff mattered. She snorted, a frustrated sound.

What the heck did it matter? Once Leo and the rest of the Mitchell family learned the truth, they'd send her packing, if they didn't kill her first. Saber in particular was one tough dude, and she wouldn't put it past him to make the hard call, get rid of the assassin. Freedom and peace of mind for all of them.

Except Leo.

Isabella fingered the tender spot where Leo had marked her. Although it had disappeared during her transformation to the male then to Gina and wasn't visible to the naked eye, it tingled beneath the surface in a stark reminder of Leo.

She knew what it meant—for her and for him. If something happened to her, Leo would be in limbo. No other mate for him. She pushed on the mark, the tiny jolt of pain bringing home the truth. By not speaking up, she'd trapped him. The back of her eyes stung as she wandered back down the footpath to Storm in a Teacup, a film of moisture obscuring her vision. Muttering a curse, she swiped away the tears and blinked for good measure. A quick deep breath to help settle her nerves and she pushed through the customer entrance of the café.

"Gina." Emily shot from behind the counter and grabbed Isabella. She clasped her in a fierce hug, arms clinging so tight Isabella could scarcely breathe. Abruptly Emily thrust her away. "Where have you been?"

Isabella took one look at Saber, who had prowled from the kitchen, and quailed. She was in big, big trouble.

"Um, I guess I'm busted," Isabella said.

The door opened and a family group entered the café, interrupting the potential scene.

Without taking his eyes off her, Saber pulled out a cell phone and hit speed dial. "Leo, Gina has arrived. Could you come and pick her up? I need to take care of a couple of things here." He disconnected and shoved the cell into his jeans pocket. "Sit and don't move until Leo comes for you."

135

"I'm sorry." The urge to cry and beg forgiveness tightened her throat, making the words difficult to squeeze free.

"We'll discuss it later." The icy tone of Saber's words showed the depths of his anger, and the knowledge made her feel even worse. In such a short time she'd come to respect and love all the Mitchells. They cared for her wellbeing and showed how pathetic her own family had been in the parenting stakes.

"I...all right." Isabella walked away to take the seat Saber had indicated. She focused on her red sneakers and wondered how to fix this mess.

A couple entered the café and Emily bustled around, taking care of their orders while Saber disappeared into the kitchen. When Isabella concentrated, she could hear the husky timbre of his voice but not his actual words.

Isabella scowled. No matter what way she looked at the situation it was difficult to see how things might improve.

Ten minutes later the door opened and Leo stepped into the café. Her heart knocked against her ribs, a new tension gripping her. She wanted to throw herself into his arms and plead with him to take her away to a private place where they could get busy. Instead, she gripped the edges of the chair base and held herself in place.

Leo scowled. "Where's Saber?"

"In the kitchen." It was a huge task to force out the reply. Her hungry gaze took in his symmetrical features, noting the strain around his mouth and the shadows beneath his eyes. Knowing she'd caused him pain made her feel even worse.

Leo strode past and disappeared out the back, returning a few minutes later. "Come on, kid. We're heading home. Saber and Emily will be back later. Until then I'm your jailer."

Isabella stood and wordlessly preceded him through the door. As far as jailers went, she could do worse. She opened the passenger door and climbed inside, buckling her seat belt while she waited for Leo. He slid behind the wheel, started up and glanced over at her.

"So, where have you been?"

"Queenstown."

"Yeah?"

To her disquiet, Isabella felt color seep into her face. She never blushed, or hadn't until she become up close and personal with Leo. "Yes." Her lips firmed to a tight line. She didn't intend to offer more information.

"Do you have a boyfriend?"

Her cheeks burned and she stared out the windscreen at the road while memories of Leo's beautiful body flickered through her mind.

"The silent treatment won't stop Saber punishing you. Ring the twins and ask them. Go on, tell me."

Isabella maintained a stubborn silence. If only he knew.

Mika booked a room at the Middlemarch Bed and Breakfast from Dunedin and arrived late evening to take up his reservation. His top lip curled as he drove along the main street of the country town. Not much to it. A café. A garage with a workshop for repairs along with petrol and diesel. The local store. A post office. School. He turned onto one of the back streets and noticed a pub not far from the railway station. A couple more accommodation places and a spot for camping rounded out the amenities.

Should be easy enough to chase up this Tomasine Brooks woman. He'd done more research and found she lived in Middlemarch. Easy to discover whatever he wanted with intellect and the resources Joseph had placed at his disposal.

Making a left turn, he did another circuit of the Middlemarch streets before pulling up outside the bed and breakfast. He switched off the ignition and reached for his cell. Ah, Isabella. He listened to the message twice before switching off the phone.

Mika opened the car door and climbed out, whistling a cheerful tune. Things were looking up, and he had Isabella worried if she was offering to work with him.

That wouldn't happen. He couldn't afford to split the price of the contract.

With this contract completed, he could walk off into the sunset with his debts paid and live happily ever after.

"You are grounded for one month."

Light punishment given the circumstances. At least Saber didn't know the truth. She'd seduced his brother and enticed him into marking her as his mate, leaving him in limbo. And worst of all, she'd placed them in danger. Mika was somewhere out there, skulking through the shadows of Middlemarch.

Isabella stomped her foot, the force of the thump darting painfully up her leg. "It's not fair. All I did was visit my friend." Might as well play a sulky sixteen-year-old.

"You lied," Saber said coldly.

"I'm going to my room." Isabella did her best grumpy, put-upon, life's-unfair impression and stomped from the room, her fists clenched at her sides.

"Dinner will be soon," Emily said.

"I'm not hungry." With ground-eating steps, she reached her bedroom and flung open the door. She stormed inside and slammed it, grinning when the loud thud echoed. Boy, this teenage stuff did have fun parts.

The humor died a rapid death while she pondered her course of action. Only one possible solution. Get her butt out there and do a search. Check the pub, the bed and breakfasts around the town plus the outlying ones, and search for anything out of the ordinary. Rental cars and vehicles from Christchurch. She hadn't done it for a while, but it was possible for chameleons to reduce to mist and seep through small gaps. Handy if she needed to break into a car or building. The problem—the process depleted her reserves, which was why she rarely used the talent.

A knock sounded on her door.

"Gina, can I come in?" Emily didn't sound angry. More worried and upset. Isabella hated that she was the cause.

"Yeah." It was difficult holding on to a teenage sulk when guilt filled her.

The door opened and Emily poked her head into the room. "Are you sure you don't want any dinner?"

"Look at me," Isabella said, gesturing at her plump body with an irritated flick of her hand. "Does it look as if missing a meal would hurt me?"

"You're a growing, healthy girl," Emily said, stepping into the bedroom. "No man likes a string bean. They want a woman they can hold, without having to worry if they squeeze too hard."

Frustration with the situation boiled up in Isabella. That she had to hide in the body of a sixteen-year-old, unable to pursue the man she loved, galled her. Pissed her off, and it did nothing for her out-of-control libido. She'd known getting close and personal with Leo before she completed the job was a mistake, but she'd let her hormones lead the way.

Mistake. Big time.

"That's not what the boys said at the party last night," Isabella snapped, making up a nonexistent party.

"Aw, honey. I'm sorry. Boys can be cruel. Remind me to tell you about my first husband when you get older. Unfortunately, some men never grow up. It's up to us to weed out the good ones."

"Like Leo," Isabella said, going for truth rather than character in her reply. Leo was a good man. Yes, he'd dated dozens of women, but most of them remained friends. He was strong and capable, and his ability to manage the vineyard had turned their Pinot Noir wine into a market leader. Yeah, as far as she was concerned, he was perfect. Apart from his stubbornness.

That would need to change.

Emily smiled. "Yes, although I think he's a bit old for you. Don't be in such a hurry to grow up, Gina. There's plenty of time for you to find a boy who understands you."

Isabella nodded while suppressing a snort. If Emily realized her true age, that she was immortal. Most chameleons died a violent death before reaching old age. It was part of the reason the race had nearly died out. They died while carrying out mercenary duties and didn't have many offspring.

"Are you sure you don't want me to bring you a tray?"

"No thanks, Emily. I'm tired. I think I'll go to sleep."

Emily's loud gasp filled the room. "You didn't—"

"No, I didn't have sex!" Isabella almost choked on the lie but must have managed a credible reply because Emily asked no more questions.

Liar, liar, her conscience mocked, but at least she didn't color and give away the truth. She'd had amazing sex with Leo. Stupendous sex, and she couldn't wait to repeat the experience.

"Ah, that's good then." Emily reached for Isabella and hugged her before kissing her on the cheek. "See you in the morning."

"I'm sorry for worrying you so much, Emily. I...I didn't think. Do you think Saber will stay mad for long?"

"I don't know. You gave us a scare, especially with a stranger wanting to know about Tomasine."

"I'd never do anything to hurt Tomasine."

"I know, honey. Sweet dreams."

The door clicked behind Emily and Isabella sighed. The web of lies kept getting thicker. She sat on the edge of her single white bed, the blue-and-white daisy-patterned cover crinkling beneath her weight. The summer sun had left a lingering heat in the room and she stood to open a window.

The action gave breath to a plan. She'd wait an hour, stuff pillows in her bed just in case Emily checked on her during the evening, and leave via the window to carry out her investigation. Saber and Leo might have extra-good hearing, but she had her own talents and stealth was one of them.

As soon as darkness fell, she pictured her Isabella image in her head and held it while she shifted. A soft glow lit her dark bedroom, giving the white lacy curtains a momentary green tinge. She suffered the slight discomfort she always felt before her body settled in the correct formation.

She grabbed her shed key and thrust it into her jacket pocket then climbed out the window. In the case of discovery, she figured it would be better to be found as a stranger rather than get Gina in trouble yet again. But lack of weapons might prove a problem. A frown puckered between her eyes. In her

Leo-addled state, she'd left her favorite blade at the cottage. Couldn't happen again, not with Mika around.

Isabella inched around the edge of the house, pausing to listen and relaxing when she heard Saber's and Emily's voices. The muted sound of the television told her Leo was watching a movie.

Relaxing a fraction, she left the shelter of the fragrant and bushy green shrub and crept around a corner, avoiding all the noise traps she'd helped Felix and Leo construct several months earlier. Using every bit of available cover she left, scanning the area in front of her.

"You going somewhere?"

Isabella froze, her heart almost leaping out her mouth. Slowly she turned to face Leo. Now here was trouble. What the fuck was she going to say in answer to his inevitable questions?

"How did you know where to find me?"

"I...ah...asked at the pub."

"Why were you leaving?"

"I...thought...ah..."

"You came to see me but you chickened out." Male satisfaction coated the words, but before she could protest, Leo grabbed her, drawing her into his embrace and holding her fast. She dragged in his scent. Her heart drummed two hard, fast beats.

She should be out there looking for Mika, trying to keep her family safe, but instead she burrowed closer and tipped up her head to invite his kiss. She tried to tell herself she was seducing him to avoid questions, that a male with sex on his mind would cause less danger to her mission.

Yeah, right. Big fat liar. She knew it, confessed to herself, but went right ahead crushing her lips to his, igniting the fire burning between them. They ate at each other's mouths, hungry and a little brutal. The pulse at her throat beat a rapid tattoo while the erotic whisper of danger laced their loving. Isabella yanked at his shirt until the metal buttons gave under the strain. She touched the bared skin greedily, pinching, kissing, biting and licking the silken warmth. Her hands went to his fly, she dragged the button open and tugged on the zipper.

"Isabella, wait," he said on a groan. "We can go inside."

No, they couldn't.

Isabella worked faster, determined to distract him. She opened the fly of his jeans, peeling the denim away to reveal his formfitting boxer shorts. With deft hands, she scooped his erection free, smoothing fingers over his satin-soft length, teasing him until he gasped and grabbed her shoulders, drawing her closer instead of pushing her away.

"We could do this in comfort," he protested.

Not gonna happen. God, she wanted him so bad. She ached, her pussy moist and more than ready for him. Hot and needy. But this time was for him. Distraction. That was all. And if she told herself that enough, maybe she'd come to believe. Forcing herself to concentrate, she sank onto her knees and took him into her mouth, licking across the swollen head, toying with his slit. His familiar taste filled her, and when she felt his hands clutch at her hair, she hummed her pleasure. Giving was as good as receiving.

Almost.

Using her hands, she scraped her nails over his balls, and with rhythmic slides of her tongue, she pushed him toward climax. She took him deeper, glancing up so she could judge how close he was to orgasm. He was watching her, the way she took him inside, the way her lips stretched around him. Her vagina clenched even as she kept up the hot, easy glides, taking him deep, licking, swallowing.

Using every weapon at her disposal to keep him off balance. With a ragged curse, he stopped fighting. He trembled, a large man under her power, giving over control to her. For an instant, she felt shame and the weight of her lies. Her rhythm faltered before she picked up again.

His balls pulled tight, and she knew he wasn't far from release. She worked his cock, made love to him, giving him everything, trying to tell him of her feelings with touch alone. He tensed and came, spurting into her mouth. Isabella swallowed until he calmed, his sigh and the loosening of the grip on her hair, letting her pull away.

Against her will, Isabella stood and stepped back. She had to peel her hands off his broad chest and clench them to fists at her side to stop herself from falling against him again. "I should go."

"Stay. Come and meet my family."

"Sorry. I need to get back to Queenstown to make my next interview."

"Then why did you come here? What are you doing creeping around?" Leo smoothed a lock of hair from her cheek, his smile slow and sexy. It made her want to grab him by his ears and mash their lips together.

It made her want so much more.

"This was a mistake. I wanted to see where you lived, to make sure you hadn't lied to me." A masterstroke of brilliance. Put everything back on him. Make it look as if she was suspicious. "My last lover lied. I needed to prove to myself that my instincts were good, that you weren't lying."

"I don't lie."

Oops, wrong tack. "No, Leo. You don't. Sorry. I...I...we...maybe this coming weekend we could meet in Queenstown again? I...as soon as you left I missed you." Isabella swallowed. "It scared me and doubts set in. I'm sorry." If he hadn't thought she was a crackpot before, he did now.

"I think I'm insulted." His gaze narrowed and irritation flushed his cheeks. "But you came and know there is no other woman."

She could hardly tell him she'd been here all the time, so she nodded. "I must go."

"How did you get here?"

Oh shoot. More questions and lies. "I borrowed a friend's motorbike."

"I'll walk you."

"It's in the town."

Silence fell. "That was a long walk."

"I told you I wasn't sure if you wanted to see me again or if it was a one-time thing between us, if you were even telling me the truth." The flare of anger she caught in Leo's countenance brought sick satisfaction. Immediately, shame filled her. Heck, she was torturing both of them with this dangerous game.

"We might not have known each other for long, but that doesn't mean I'm not serious. Did you see me sending you away? Hell, I want to introduce you to my family. Doesn't that tell you how serious I am?"

"Yes. I'm sorry for doubting you." She seemed to be apologizing a lot today. And then there was the matter of his mark, the one she wore on her flesh. The one that tingled each time she fingered it. "I'm embarrassed. Please, can I meet your family another time?"

Leo took her hand, but she didn't think he bought her lame excuse, not judging by his tense stance. "Wait by my SUV. I'll give you a ride. Just let me grab my keys and tell my brother where I'm going."

Isabella gave a jerky nod, knowing the second he left her alone she would shift to leopard and race into town. She couldn't risk the truth coming out yet, not until she found and disposed of Mika. Once again her heart ached at the deception, but she couldn't see any other way. If he changed his mind and dragged her inside, she'd have a problem.

Heart thudding and nerves prickling, she watched Leo disappear into the darkness. She shifted, grimacing at the shift of bones and flesh, the sharp pull and hint of pain before she dropped to all fours. She padded away, increasing her speed once clearing the garden.

Isabella ran, leaving a little part of her soul behind.

Chapter 10

Gone

She'd left.

Leo cursed long and loud before hustling to his SUV. He should have trusted gut instinct and dragged her inside the house. Something smelled, and it wasn't just her fishy story.

She couldn't have walked far.

He'd catch her and grill her for the truth this time. Lifting his head, he attempted to locate her scent. Lavender. The moist earth from Emily's garden. Trees. Plants. Fresh air.

Not a single scent out of place. How was that possible? He could smell her on him but no trail led from where they'd stood together. A human. Hell, he was feeling like a convenience food—available on demand.

Leo palmed his pockets for his keys and realized that in his hurry he'd left them on the kitchen counter. "Fuck!" Nothing about this romance came easy. He stomped back inside and couldn't find his keys. He thumped and cursed again.

"Problem?" Saber appeared from the lounge.

"Yes, there's a problem," Leo snarled.

Emily darted to Saber's side, and Leo caught her blink at his tone.

"She's gone. I can't find my keys."

"Really?" Emily asked. "That can't be right. Women never say no to you. You don't suffer from rejection."

"Don't laugh," Leo snapped when he noticed her quivering bottom lip. If she laughed, he would too. Not grumpy by nature, he wanted to stay angry at Isabella. The next time they saw each other they'd talk—he'd make sure of it—before they took off their clothes and did anything hot, heavy and fun.

Dammit, Isabella possessed secrets. Answers—he needed them, because if he'd learned one thing from this latest debacle, it was they were right for each other. Isabella felt it, but for some reason was running scared. Yeah, he'd explain things to her, tell her what he was and what it meant. He'd tie her up if necessary. A smile bloomed at the thought of his lover incapacitated with ropes, his to do with as he willed. Damn if that didn't sound fine. He'd bind her to his bed and keep her there until submission and truth spilled from her sexy lips.

And he bore a matching mark on his body. At present, he didn't care about the location. He wanted her to acknowledge their bond, accept it.

"I don't like that smile," Saber said. "Looks like trouble."

"I won't be the one in trouble," Leo retorted.

"Your keys are in the lounge," Emily said. "I'll get them."

"How did she manage to get so close to the house without us hearing? With the warning systems in place, we should have heard a stranger arrive. Do you want me to come with you?" Saber waited for his decision.

"Thanks, but I need to do this on my own."

"You'll ring if you need help?" Emily asked, handing him his keys and his cell phone.

Leo smiled at her, feeling calmer now. He and Isabella might laugh about this in a few years. Something to tell their children. Their grandchildren. "Count on it."

He stalked out the door and jumped into his SUV, speeding along the gravel driveway to hit the main road. She couldn't have gone far.

Not true, he discovered. Although he scanned the road, he reached the town without seeing Isabella.

Isabella raced straight to the shed where she kept her bike because she also stored a cache of weapons there. She shifted, located the key she'd placed in her pocket earlier and unlocked the door before slipping inside. Secured and hidden from the casual searcher, her spare weapons would save her butt this time. Although skilled in hand-to-hand combat, she preferred a weapon that allowed her distance from her target.

She climbed up into a concealed crawl space in the ceiling and stretched out to grab a cloth-covered package. Back on the ground, she unwrapped the parcel and pulled out a knife, testing it for weight. Perfect. She slid it into her boot and stuffed one of the smaller guns in the inside jacket pocket of her leather jacket. Ordinarily she'd take her case containing her sniper rifle but it was still at the cottage. Bloody Leo's fault for distracting her.

Armed again, she left the shed and checked out the bed and breakfast places in the town. Frankly, she couldn't imagine Mika staying at the campground because he had a taste for the finer things in life. If he was here in Middlemarch, as her gut told her, then his nose was wrinkling at the family-style accommodation.

She slinked down the road, keeping to the deep shadows so the few people driving past didn't notice her. The first place she tried had a family staying, and they drove a van to fit in the kids and their toys. Definitely not Mika. When she approached the second bed and breakfast, the one opposite the petrol station, she saw a new-model rental car.

"This is more like it," she muttered. "But do you come from Christchurch?" With one eye searching for approaching vehicles, she prowled around the sedan and tried the passenger door. Locked. Isabella peered through the windscreen but couldn't see inside the vehicle to prove Mika's presence.

A vehicle approached and she backed away from the rental, ducking into the deep shadows cast by a hedge. Her eyes widened when she identified the driver.

"Leo." Her nipples drew tight, her thoughts diverting to sex. She shook her head, part of her wanting to step into the path of his vehicle and have her way with him. Again. Now that she'd touched him intimately, she couldn't wait to run her hands over him again, take his cock in her mouth and drive him crazy. Drive them both crazy.

She wanted to try everything. Toys. Definitely toys. Yeah, she'd love to bind the man's hands, his feet, and have him under her control. For this man she'd dress up in a little maid's costume, anything to keep him in her bed. *It would be her pleasure.*

Isabella shook herself free from the sensual spell and shifted her weight, feeling the dampness between her thighs. This was not a good time for her to go head-to-head with Leo. Not a good time.

The SUV continued past in the direction of the pub. Her breath eased out with relief as she turned her attention back to the vehicle. Nothing inside the sedan to help her.

Security lights lit the garden area in front of the bed and breakfast. She'd visited the place with Emily to deliver baked goods for a party and knew the location of the bedrooms. One was around the back—a double room—and a second guest bedroom was to the left of the building. Isabella considered shifting to a bird or another creature but decided it would be too slow to shift back to human to access her weapons again.

With another glance both left and right, she hurried to the neighboring property and vaulted the fence. Just as she'd landed on the other side of the low hedge-lined fence another vehicle passed, but to her relief it kept going without slowing. She could do without a nosy bystander accusing her of being a Peeping Tom or worse.

After waiting an instant longer, she crept along the edge of the hedge and the boundary fence running between the property and the bed and breakfast. She squeezed through a gap and slipped behind a big tree. The trunk felt smooth beneath the palms of her hands as she peeked from behind her cover. The rooms lay in darkness.

An elderly couple occupied the first bedroom. She could make out the man's bald head and the woman's tight gray curls. Isabella skulked along the exterior wall of the house until she could peer into the other guest bedroom. A single person. The hair color looked damn close to Mika's. She willed the person to turn over and puffed out a frustrated breath when they didn't move. She scanned the room, searching for clues. Ah! A slow smile curled across her lips. She'd recognize that bag anywhere. It was the one Mika had carried onto the plane at the Queenstown airport.

Isabella retreated, knowing she could hardly barge into the bed and breakfast at this time of the night. Finding the time to confront Mika might prove a problem since Saber and Emily had caught her in a lie.

She retreated, taking care not to draw attention while worrying about how to protect the Mitchell family.

"What the hell do you think you're doing?" A masculine hand bracketed her wrist, holding her in place.

Angry at her lapse in concentration, she turned to face Leo. This was gonna be good. She was out of lies. "I—"

"Don't bother, sweetheart. I'd prefer to wait until we're somewhere private. We'll talk then."

Earlier his words would've thrilled her, but now...now they held steely intent. This time she wouldn't be able to talk her way out, not unless she could trick him.

Isabella walked at his side, mind working busily. God, she loved him. Loved him so much it hurt.

He'd parked his SUV farther down the road, which was why she hadn't heard it stop. They reached the vehicle and Leo stopped by the passenger door. He unlocked it with an automatic opener, the soft peep sounding more like a key locking than a door opening. Her heart slammed against her ribs. She couldn't tell him yet. Not before she knew for sure the last threat of danger was over.

"Get in."

She hadn't witnessed this side of Leo. There was more of Saber in him than she'd thought. She'd underestimated him, despite knowing him well, and it wouldn't happen again. Lifting her nose into the air and letting him hear her indignant sniff, she slid into the passenger seat.

Leo rounded the SUV and climbed behind the steering wheel. Isabella had a chance to escape since he hadn't relocked the door after her but she remained motionless, debating the best course of action. Then it was too late because the door locked.

"Put on your seat belt."

Isabella obeyed, feeling a ripple of arousal shoot straight to her pussy. She took a quick breath, amazed at her reaction. Control was part of her character makeup. If a mercenary ceded command of a situation, they weren't good at their job. She was—excellent, which was why Tomasine was alive and Mika remained the sole mercenary still on the job.

Leo drove out of town and turned onto a side road leading to the river. He switched off the engine. Silence rippled between them, palpable and scary. She licked her lips, attempting to dispel the dryness. Nerves jiggled inside her stomach, and this surprised her. Normally, she remained rock solid.

"You going to tell me what's going on?"

"I'd prefer not to."

Leo shifted in the driver's seat. "Felix told me that one day I'd meet someone who'd drive me to distraction. A woman who didn't pay attention to my looks." He dragged a hand through his dark hair, ruffling the curls and making her want to smooth them. "Why couldn't I have fallen for one of them? Tell me, Isabella. And don't give me crap about a job. I'm adding facts and coming up with alarming answers."

Isabella hesitated. She'd need to give him the truth, or at least a partial version. "I don't work in a hotel."

"And?"

"I don't want to put you in danger." Well, that was the truth.

"Do I look like a powder puff to you?" he demanded. "I'm capable of looking after myself."

Ooh, tetchy. She took a deep breath and gave him more. "I'm a mercenary."

"You're the blonde," Leo said in a hard voice.

At least he hadn't hit her or laughed in her face. She patted her brown hair, a smile flirting with the corners of her lips. "Last time I looked in the mirror I had plain old brown."

"Don't insult my intelligence."

"Ooh! More than a pretty face." The second the words left her mouth she wanted to recall them.

"Out," Leo ordered. He opened the door. "We're going for a walk."

Alarm skittered through her veins. "Why?"

"Because we haven't finished talking, sweetheart."

She'd never seen him like this, face devoid of humor, his green eyes dark and stormy, glittering with temper. Her mouth became even drier, flutters of both fear and sexual arousal mingling. Surely he wouldn't try to hurt her? Not that she'd blame him...

"Don't look at me like that." The snarl in his voice brought another spiral of alarm.

"Okay." She opened the SUV door.

A breeze lightened the stifling summer heat, ruffling her shoulder-length hair. Isabella rounded the SUV. A half-moon hung in the sky, the light it shed enough to soften the darkness. Leo followed suit and gestured for her to walk with him along the river edge. Although they weren't touching, she could feel the tension in him, the tamped anger.

157

They walked in silence for five minutes until she decided enough. She came to an abrupt halt. "Ask your questions. I'll answer them if I can."

"If you can?"

"There is more going on here than you could understand."

"Tell me." When she hesitated, he took half a step and halted without touching her. His face softened. "I can't help if you won't talk."

But if she told him everything, it would place him in danger. He'd want to help. Her mouth tightened to a stubborn line. Take over in typical Mitchell fashion. Besides, she worried about how Leo would react if he learned why she was hanging around Middlemarch, if he learned she killed for a living.

"I can't," she whispered, the ache of longing tightening around her chest.

"Can't or won't." The hard, emotionless Leo returned.

"Don't you understand? This isn't a game. People might get hurt."

"I imagine mercenaries get injured."

"They die," Isabella said in a flat tone. "That's why it's dangerous."

Leo frowned then shifted tack. "Are you the blonde?"

Isabella sighed before deciding to give him the truth. "Yes, I'm the blonde."

With a quick move, Leo closed the distance between them, his hands clamped around her biceps, holding her firm. "And exactly when had you intended to let me in on that little secret?"

His warm breath wafted across her face. With every inhalation, she dragged in his familiar scent. Enticing, seductive Leo. More than enough to distract her from her mission. The thought added steel to her spine, something lacking during the last days.

"I don't know you well. Do you go around telling your deepest secrets to a person you've just met?" A good conversation salvo, and one he couldn't dispute. He hadn't told her he was a feline shifter.

Leo stared at her, the intense green of his gaze making her wish she could read his mind. Unfortunately, not part of the chameleon talent pool.

His hands flexed on her upper arms, his chest rose during a deep breath. "Is there any immediate danger?"

"Not right now." But maybe tomorrow. Mika needed to gather information. He wouldn't find Tomasine, but he'd learn about the Mitchells and assume they were hiding her. Then he'd make his move. "But there will be danger."

Leo nodded, not taking his eyes off her face. "We'll talk to Saber tomorrow. Saber is my brother."

"Okay." Isabella turned to go.

Leo tightened his grasp on her arms. "Not so fast," he whispered. "We have things to settle between us. You're staying right here where I can watch you. I don't want you to disappear again."

"But—" Isabella broke off when she realized her predicament. If she didn't get back to the house and change to her Gina persona, Emily and Saber would worry. They'd think she'd run away, and if she stayed with Leo, the family would face danger at Mika's hands.

Leo didn't understand how dangerous the mercenary could be, especially with the money Joseph had put on Tomasine's head.

"What do you intend to do with me? Turn me in to the authorities? I break the law when I kill people."

"How many people have you killed?" Leo's expression conveyed neither disgust nor approval. Once again, she failed to read him and it irritated her. Normally, she was an expert in body language.

"A good assassin doesn't boast of their hits." Even though it was her job, her sole talent, each kill left blood on her, a stain she couldn't remove no matter how often she soaped her hands.

"Hell, I don't believe this."

"What? You think mercenaries are all big, stocky men and ex-military? Not true. A mercenary blends and doesn't fit stereotypes." She sure as hell didn't.

"I don't want to talk anymore."

Her shoulders slumped. Pain gripped her but she forced it away. She had a mission to complete. She didn't require his approval.

Turning away, Leo stalked back to his SUV. He was leaving.

Isabella sank down until she sat on a log, the back of her eyes aching with unshed tears. She swallowed, breathing carefully to control her emotions. Damn, she hadn't expected him to leave, but understood even though it hurt like hell. Yep, looked as if she was destined to walk alone.

Yet again.

Without a man in the picture, she'd have to concentrate on the job. Probably better all around. She squeezed her eyes closed and walked through everything she'd need to do tomorrow. A way to control her wayward emotions.

The touch of a hand on the top of her head made her start. Her eyes snapped open and she sprang to her feet, knife sliding from her boot.

"Whoa!" Leo dropped the blanket he carried under one arm and lifted both hands up in a sign of surrender.

Isabella lowered the knife. "Sorry. It's not good to creep up on me."

"No kidding," Leo said with a wry laugh. "I said I didn't intend to talk, but that didn't mean I was leaving. I thought we could do something else instead. Can I come closer without you gutting me?"

"Yeah." She slid the weapon back into her boot and stood silent, and unsure of herself. "Um...what did you have in mind?"

"I want to make love to you. I need to fill you and make you scream."

A smile bloomed without warning. "You're full of yourself."

"I'm crazy about you, Isabella." Leo closed the distance between them and smoothed the hair off her face.

"Even though I'm a mercenary?"

"It depends on who you're stalking. If it's one of my family, then we have a problem. Since you've admitted you're the mystery blonde I suspect you're not after a family member."

"I don't know your family," Isabella lied. She'd lay down her life for any of them. She could never repay their kindness. *Never*. But that didn't stop her from trying.

"Then why were you skulking around our house?"

"I thought you didn't want to talk," Isabella countered.

"I don't, but this is a postponement. We'll talk soon."

Before Isabella could react, he lowered his head to kiss her. Despite his gentle grip on her shoulders, his kiss held an edge of anger. He savaged her mouth, taking rather than giving. She understood, accepted how her skulking appeared to a bystander, how her actions and refusal to speak gave rise to suspicion.

Leo scraped his teeth along the cords of her neck, lashed his tongue across the mark he'd placed on her earlier and wetness pooled between her thighs. *Her mate. All hers.*

In the past, she'd never coveted possessions, never needed a man in her life, but now she understood everyone needed someone, a person to give a damn.

He bit down on the mark, offering the sharp bite of teeth. Her pulse spiked, the liquid roll of desire tugging deep in her pussy. She softened, melted into his larger frame. His scent swirled through her, dark and rich. *Hers*. All hers. Take the final step. Sharp canines pushed free, protruded beneath her top lip and panic arced to life in her. *Not now. No, she had to control it*.

He removed her boots, pulled out her knife and set it aside. He stood again, kissed her hard. Masculine hands ripped at her clothes, paused when he came to her gun and another knife. Soon, the cool night air brushed her breasts. He rose to spread the blanket on a soft spot of the riverbank.

"Lie down," he ordered.

Isabella obeyed, granting him the liberty and the façade of control. Her way of apologizing. In the future, if they had one, he wouldn't find her so biddable. She stared while he disrobed, taking in long muscular legs, his smooth, wide chest and the muscles that rippled across his stomach. He peeled his boxers away from his cock, his shaft springing free.

Her breathing went shallow and she realized a predatory smile had formed on her lips. Maybe she wasn't giving away as much control as she'd thought. The need to conquer still throbbed through her and the realization she needed a strong man to counter her rough edges.

Leo Mitchell was that man. She knew it, had always known it, but she also knew she'd have to prove herself to him. She expected nothing less.

"Looking good," she whispered, letting desire shine from her eyes. *Hiding nothing.* "Every time I look at you, I want you more. You're addictive, Leo."

"And yet you hide from me," he murmured. "You don't trust me." His voice held pain.

"I...it's hard for me," Isabella said. "Trusting. I haven't...I don't have a good track record." As much truth as she could give him. An ache formed at the back of her eyes, and in astonishment, she realized it wouldn't take much to tip her over into tearful. She swallowed, hardly able to imagine crying, let alone tears falling down her face.

"One day you can tell me about it." Leo closed the distance between them until they were a hairsbreadth away from each other.

Silence fell, and it throbbed, thick with tension. Isabella fought a whimper, another anomaly for her. They showered on her hard and fast.

Leo reached for her again with a savage edge, his strong fingers threading through her hair to hold her still while he ravished her lips. His thumb strummed across her mark, each slow pass ratcheting up the hunger building inside her. He kissed her for a long time before he deepened the contact.

Gasping, she pulled away, dragging drafts of air into her starved lungs. He might have drawn back, but still he touched and stroked her mark, pushing her into dangerous territory. She wanted so badly to take the next step.

Her stomach hollowed with the strength of her need, her hips canting toward him. Her breasts felt swollen, achy while slick moisture between her thighs told of her readiness to take him.

The seal of ownership, of promises and mating was powerful. It sucked at her free will, pushing, pushing, *pushing*. Driving her to confess.

Isabella shook her head, a silent warning to herself. *Don't do it. It's too soon.*

Leo moved without warning, covering her body, pinning her to the ground. Panting she lay facedown, her nose rubbing the rough weave of the blanket. Tense and aroused. Finally, he ceased rubbing his thumb over the mark.

Isabella let out a sigh of relief, glad of the respite. She dragged in a slow breath, but it emphasized the way her body throbbed, her skin stretched tight and sensitive.

His penis brushed her backside, nudging at the valley between the rounded globes. He leaned some of his weight onto her, rubbing against the tattoo of the small green dragon at the small of her back. She gasped, lust roaring through her. She wriggled, feeling empty, desperately needing his thick cock to fill her.

"Take me," she whispered. "Please."

"Do you belong to me?" he demanded, arrogant in his commands.

She didn't care. All she wanted, needed, desired was his cock hammering into her, a release from the tension holding her in thrall.

"Do you?"

"Yes."

"Louder. I didn't hear you."

"I need you Leo, and I want you. No one else. Only you."

He didn't answer, but his grip lightened, the press of fingers around her biceps lessening. His large body shifted, his cock pushing against the crease of her ass. Her pussy fluttered, the emptiness emphasized.

She groaned a sound of protest, but he whispered to her. Dark and nasty words against her ear before his tongue swiped across the mark. Through a heavy fog of desire, she struggled to move, wanting to face him, to touch and be touched in return. He resisted the attempt, instead urging her to part her legs for him.

The night air was cool on her damp, fevered flesh. Suppressed tension vibrated through her. His hands shaped her form, curved around her hips and arranged her to his satisfaction. On fours, she trembled, wondered how long he'd make her wait. Punishment. Oh, she understood the concept, but that didn't mean she had to enjoy it.

He backed away until he no longer touched, leaving her waiting, wondering.

A sharp slap across her backside gave her the answer. It surprised a cry from her, although it hadn't hurt.

"That's for lying," he said, his voice dark with satisfaction.

A second blow struck her, lower and surprisingly arousing. Her flesh heated, tingled.

"That's for sneaking around."

Another blow. A different angle. Different intensity and close to her aching pussy.

"That's for running off."

He struck again until her bottom smarted, her skin throbbed and the arousal taunting, pushing her up into new heights of pleasure. Expecting yet another smack, he surprised her by curling his hand around one breast. He plucked at the nipple, tugging, rolling. Alternatively giving pain and pleasure. Soon her nipple throbbed in time with her bottom.

Isabella could've moved, could have fought him, but she submitted and prayed he'd give her relief soon because she felt as if she might explode.

But he didn't hurry. Seemed he had his own agenda, one he didn't care to share with her. He stroked her mark, traced her green dragon with his tongue, sometimes alone. Sometimes in tandem. He smacked her backside without warning, warming the cooling skin and keeping her on edge. The scent of her arousal filled the air. He understood what he was doing to her, the torture he layered on her sensitive, aroused body.

"Leo," she wailed. "Take me. I said I was sorry. Please. No more."

"But, sweetheart, I'm just starting."

That was what she feared. He intended to strip her emotions bare, leaving her vulnerable and needy.

"But I don't have all night."

"Did you intend to go somewhere?" The silky voice held a sliver of menace.

"No. No, not going anywhere." Not until he did something about the ache gnawing at her body. "But if you don't hurry, I might take matters into my own hands."

"Ah, but, Isabella, where's the fun in that? Won't the wait be worth it?"

"No."

Leo chuckled. "Maybe we could go faster."

Her head drooped, relief at his concession letting her relax. But he didn't go faster. It was a lie. A ploy to drive her to madness. He cupped her buttocks, ran his finger down the crease between, pausing to tease her rosette. Her pussy clenched, her jaw echoing the move.

"That is not fast," she dared to complain.

He pushed her legs farther apart until she was open and exposed.

"Your pretty pink folds are glistening."

"That's because I'm ready for you to fuck me," she snapped.

"Now. Now. Patience, Isabella." The sharp smack across her buttocks echoed in the still night.

"Ow, that hurt."

"Not as much as I'd like to hurt you."

The darkness in his tone sparked a shard of fear before she realized he was all threats. She knew Leo, knew that while he might be a little rough, he would never hurt her. She trusted him, which begged the question of why she hadn't confessed her true purpose. The words tickled her lips, but she choked them back. Instead, she waggled her butt. Maybe she could tempt him.

He laughed, but not before she heard a soft groan. The stroke of his fingers over her dragon tattoo sent a spike of pleasure to her clit. Then she felt it—the warm lap of his tongue, the rough rasp of her sensitive skin.

A groan broke free, low and needy.

He used his fingers to tease her rosette, back and forth, dark pleasure heating her body. He lapped her juices, smoothing the slickness from her weeping entrance and across her swollen bud. Leo pushed his finger into her anus, piercing the dark hole while his tongue swept down, thrusting into her vagina as far as he could. A ripple of pleasure speared her, nerve endings pulsing with delight.

"Leo, please. I need your cock."

Thankfully, this time he listened. He pulled back, leaving her pulsing, empty, then pierced her with his shaft, pushing deep into her channel, filling her to capacity. With hard digs, he rocked into her, feeling bigger than ever before. Heat and pressure rampaged through her, and when he leaned over, pressing his chest against her back to grasp the mark with his sharp teeth, she lost it. Bucking frantically, orgasm thundered through her, a cry of pleasure echoing in the lonely night. With a convulsive heave of muscles, Leo followed her into climax, his cock flexing, rippling while her pussy hungrily clenched his breadth. Her chest heaved with the need for air, the hot sex between them making her feel alive.

Leo pulled from her, and when she glanced over her shoulder, she noticed his glistening cock. He was still aroused, hard. No condom. Not that it mattered in the scheme of things. She thought he might mention it but he didn't. His features shone with intent, purpose.

"This time I want to see your breasts," he said, the husky note in his voice making her pussy twitch. He rolled onto the blanket and looked up at her in challenge. "Take me, ride me and make me come again."

Isabella trembled, wondering if she'd hide the emotions that might give away her thoughts. His night vision was good. He'd see everything. But then maybe it wouldn't matter. Maybe it would lull his suspicions and give her an opportunity to leave. Slowly Isabella straddled his hips and rubbed her pussy against his groin.

"That's it, sweetheart. You're nice and wet. You can take me again."

Not only could she take him but she wanted him. Isabella gripped his dick, fisting him and teasing him to full erection. She cupped his balls, fondling them until his breathing grew harsh. With trembling fingers, she guided him to her, savoring the hot, wet slide as he filled her again. She rode him at a steady pace until the ball of heat inside her threatened to detonate. She watched every flicker of emotion on his face, in his green eyes.

"Perfect," he said, his words not much more than a groan.

Isabella pinched her nipple before sliding her fingers downward to pleasure herself.

"I enjoy the way you do that."

But he disliked her secrets. Her fingers slid across her achy clit, her body swaying as she rode him. The wet sound of arousal, of hot sex didn't stop her enjoyment. Instead, her finger moved faster, circling her nub, passing over it. Her pussy pulsed, and his growl of pleasure pleased her.

He rose upward to meet her as she surged down, their bodies slapping together, taking their lovemaking into another territory. Fast. Urgent. Full of groans and pleasured cries. Her stomach tightened, and she hovered for an instant before fracturing into pleasure. A heartbeat later, he joined her, his hard thrusts jolting her body, prolonging her climax until every last sensation faded.

Isabella collapsed into his arms, never this relaxed or at such peace. Maybe she'd have a short nap. She was vaguely aware of Leo separating their sweaty bodies before he gathered her close again. Love for Leo filled her, wrapping around her heart and soul, but she didn't say a word. She couldn't with the secrets between them.

Chapter 11

Danger

"Isabella, it's time for us to leave." Leo shook his mate gently, and unable to resist, brushed a kiss across her bare shoulder. He wanted to love her again but this morning, the questions between them created a wall. He needed truth.

Her gorgeous eyes flicked open, and she became instantly awake. A mercenary who shot to kill. Leo couldn't believe she'd hurt his family, not his mate, so he clung to the fragile trust hovering between them. Instinct told him there was more to her story.

"What are you going to do?" She remained motionless, and Leo saw the tension creeping through her muscles.

"Come and meet my family. Have breakfast with me."

A flash of panic, too quick for him to decipher, hit her face. She stiffened before pushing away. "Another time. I need to check a few things this morning."

"I'll come with you."

"I—"

"Why don't you just tell me to take a hike?" Her rejection made his chest ache and started his mind whirring. Did she have someone else? Was he a bit on the side? Someone to pass the time between jobs?

"It's better if I do this on my own. Can we meet later?" Her bright smile didn't reassure him. The minute he left, she'd disappear, and he'd be lucky if he saw her again. Dammit, he loved her. She was his mate and he couldn't let her go without a fight. "This afternoon?" Her gaze skittered in his direction but didn't settle.

Yeah, right. Leo shrugged. "Sure. Whatever."

"Drop me in town by the café."

Leo pulled away from her warm body and stood. He grabbed his clothes and dressed. Isabella rolled, climbing to her feet in a graceful manner and turned away to pick up her clothes and dress. It pissed him off—the way she could act as if there were nothing between them.

"You ready to go now?" Sarcasm laced his words, but she didn't react. Nothing unusual. He was coming to realize she was self-contained and didn't give away her emotions unless that was her intention.

"Yeah."

She headed back to his SUV, her hips swaying, drawing his attention. Leo brushed past ferns and stepped over a fallen log, his mind on Isabella. There had to be a way to move on with this relationship, get her to trust him with the truth.

Her version of the truth.

His gut told him she wasn't a bad person since his feline had claimed her. Leo dug into the rear pocket of his jeans to grab his keys, unlocked the vehicle and climbed inside. Isabella joined him and he started the SUV and backed up, doing a three-point turn.

The drive back to town took place in silence. Suddenly, Isabella stiffened, her breath exiting with a hiss.

"I need you to follow that rental car," she ordered. "Don't get too close, but don't lose it."

"Who is it?"

"My friend Mika."

"Mika? The guy you met up with in the casino?"

"Yeah."

Leo heard the tense note in her voice. "Who is he?"

"Mercenary."

"After Tomasine?"

"So it would seem."

"We need to tell Saber." Leo turned his attention back to the rental car.

"No, I'm handling it."

"What are you going to do? Shoot him?"

"Yes."

The abrupt reply brought the truth home more than seeing the gun in her hand or learning of her occupation.

"Did you shoot the guy they found a couple of days ago? Who is paying you? And why are you after Mika?"

"I don't want to discuss it."

The rental car headed out of town and turned onto the road leading to his family house. Isabella ducked out of sight.

Leo frowned. "What are you doing?"

"I don't want Mika to discover me here. It will put him on guard. I want him focused on his target, not me."

Her answer didn't reassure him, but at least Tomasine and her daughter's location remained a secret from all apart from immediate family and the council. The rental car pulled over to the side of the road and stopped.

"Keep going. Don't stop. I don't want him to become suspicious."

Leo drove past and once they'd rounded a corner and the rental car was no longer in sight, Isabella unfastened her seat belt, opened the door.

"What the hell are you doing? Shut the damn door."

"I'm getting out here. I need to track Mika. Go home so he doesn't get suspicious."

"But—"

Before he could finish his protest, Isabella leaped from the moving vehicle. Acute fear struck him until he saw her roll and dart into the undergrowth.

"Fuck," he breathed, his hands tightening on the steering wheel. Leo wanted to stomp on the brakes, grab the woman and tan her backside for scaring him so much. But he also needed to warn his family. He'd never been so torn.

With another curse, he pressed on the accelerator and headed for home.

Emily and Saber were in the kitchen when he strode inside.

"Leo, Gina with you?" Saber asked.

"No, I haven't seen her. Just arrived home. Isn't she here?"

"Her pillows are stuffed under the blankets to make it appear she's present." Emily's voice broke, and she sounded close to tears. "I think she's run away. Saber is going out to look for her."

"I'm afraid we have other problems right now. I found Isabella again last night, and we spent the night together."

"Why don't you bring her inside and introduce us?" Emily asked.

"Because I found out she's the mystery blonde who saved Sylvie when she went missing. She's here on the trail of a mercenary. Hell." Leo dragged his hand through his hair. "My mate Isabella is a mercenary."

"Whose side is she on?" Saber asked, cutting to the heart.

"I'm not sure." Fuck, Leo had no idea if he should trust his instincts. "No clue, but the other mercenary is looking for Tomasine. Isabella didn't say but I suspect he's the one who rang wanting to speak with Tomasine. By now he'll have learned she married Felix, which is why we passed him on the way out here."

Emily gasped. "He's here?"

"Yeah, and I know you're worried, but it's best that she's not here while this guy is skulking around."

Saber shot him a sharp glance. "You said we. Where's Isabella?"

"She's out hunting him." Leo's stomach clenched. He needed to be with Isabella. "I'm going back out now. I wanted to warn you first."

"You should go too," Emily said to Saber. "And maybe you're right about Gina, but that won't stop me worrying. I'm going to ring around her friends. When I find that girl, she's in big trouble. Grounded for three months at least."

"No," Leo said. "I don't think Emily should be left alone. This guy is a professional. He'll want to extract information and he won't care how he gets it."

Saber gave a quick nod. "You going in feline form?"

"Yeah, it's quicker."

"Take care, Leo." Saber grasped his shoulder and squeezed. "If he's an assassin, he'll have a weapon."

Leo ripped off his T-shirt and shucked his jeans, grinning as Saber clapped his hand over Emily's eyes. He strode outside and shifted to leopard, letting out a low grunt of farewell before he hurtled along the driveway and jumped over the fence into the paddock. When he neared the rental car, he slowed, paused to listen. Someone walked in the paddock below the road. He didn't think it was Isabella because the footsteps sounded heavier than hers.

"Going somewhere, Mika?"

Leo crawled up to the fence on his stomach and peered over the road into the paddock below. Mika stood fifty feet from

Isabella. The look on the male's face matched his own surprise. How the hell had Isabella crept up without him sensing her?

Mika recovered rapidly, his hand hanging at his side. He might pretend to be relaxed but Leo sensed the other male's tension.

"What are you doing here?" Mika asked, aiming for pleasant.

Leo cursed. He needed to get closer to help. In that moment he trusted his mate. He hadn't been sure until now. She'd saved Sylvie, and she'd had the chance to go straight to the house to nail Tomasine. She hadn't. Instead, she was here facing Mika.

"What? You haven't figured it out yet?" Isabella mocked.

"You want the hit," Mika said. "I should have suspected when you offered the information that the queen and her child were in Auckland."

"They are in Auckland."

Leo took a chance and jumped the fence, landing silently on the other side. Neither of the mercenaries spared him a glance.

Mika advanced, still relaxed, as if he thought he could take her in a fight. "If they're in Auckland, why are you here? I ask myself this question, Isabella. What the hell sort of game are you playing?"

Leo wanted the same answer. Although he'd given his trust, he hated not knowing the plan. This was his mate, and she was in danger. Instinct drove him to protect her. His lip curled up in a snarl and his tail flicked from side to side, agitation bleeding out in the equivalent of toe-tapping.

Just his luck to mate with a woman who didn't need protection. A mercenary for fuck's sake. A low rumble of irritation escaped until he realized he risked giving his presence away. The noise ceased, and he crawled closer, thankful for the rock outcroppings that gave him cover.

"No games, Mika. I don't play games. This is a job like any other."

"Why haven't you checked in? Everyone thought you were dead."

Isabella snorted. "I'm a self-employed contractor, working on my own. I do the job the way I see fit."

"You've changed. Grown soft. Fuck, you've fallen for a guy."

Even Leo saw the flash of emotion on Isabella's face, and he wasn't near the couple. His tail stilled and satisfaction filled him. *His mate.* Once he got her back to the house, they'd talk. No more secrets.

"My private life is not your concern," she said in a cool voice.

"This hit is mine." Mika grabbed a gun from inside his jacket and fired. The shot echoed as Isabella let out a hoarse shout. She grabbed her knife from her boot and fired it at Mika.

A strike.

Mika's second shot went wild. Leo sprang from cover with a ferocious snarl, charging the couple. He watched Isabella waver and drop to the ground. Mika fled, heading for his vehicle.

No contest. Leo let him go and ran to Isabella's side. He heard the rapid departure of the rental vehicle as he shifted to human form and kneeled beside her. A steady pulse. Still alive. Blood seeped from a wound in her chest.

The bastard had hit her at close range.

"Come on, sweetheart. Stay with me." Leo picked her up and ran toward the house as fast as he could. He clutched her close, fear riding him at her unconscious state.

Saber must have heard his crashing progress. The front door flew open and Leo sprinted inside, clutching his precious burden.

"She's been shot. The mercenary."

"Take her into your room," Emily said. "I'll get the first-aid kit."

Leo placed her on his bed and removed her leather jacket. She stirred, groaning as he ripped her cotton shirt to expose the bullet wound. Saber came up behind him to stare over his shoulder. As they studied the wound, Isabella's flesh rippled, and the bullet worked its way out.

"Holy shit," Saber said in awe. "What is she?"

"Smells human," Leo said, blinking when the flesh knit, closing Isabella's wound. She sighed but didn't wake.

"Not human, bro, but pretty."

"Mine," Leo snarled, clasping one pale feminine hand in a statement of possession.

Saber laughed and backed up to give Leo space, his hands raised in surrender. "Not arguing the point. I have Emily."

"Sorry," Leo mumbled. "I—"

"Once the mating process is complete life becomes easier."

A feminine scream jerked their attention from Isabella.

"Emily!" Saber disappeared from his room in the blink of an eye. Another scream and a masculine snarl prodded Leo into action. He sprinted down the hall, coming to an abrupt halt. Mika had Emily, a gun pressed against her temple.

Saber growled, a low sound that made the hairs at the back of Leo's neck prickle. His gut jumped, fear and adrenaline attempting to punch holes in his chest. He'd watched Mika shoot his mate with no apparent regret. The man's mean expression told Leo he'd have no compunction in killing Emily.

"What do you want?" Saber's green eyes glinted with icy control.

Leo turned his attention to Mika and Emily. His sister-in-law bristled with anger rather than succumbing to tremors of fear.

"Where can I find Tomasine Brooks?" Mika asked.

Saber appeared to relax. "Why?"

"She has information I require."

"What sort of information?" Leo asked.

"Don't come any closer," Mika snapped. "I'll shoot her."

"Hiding behind a female." Leo shook his head. "Not cool for a tough dude."

"I meant it," Mika snarled. "No closer."

Saber stepped back. "We don't know the person you're looking for. Let Emily go."

"Don't lie. The locals call her Peeping Tom. She married your brother. I just want to talk to her."

"You could have rung and made an appointment," Leo said. "That's what normal people do." At least the man didn't realize Tomasine was the very person he was searching for and wanted to kill.

A soft sound—a footstep—attracted Leo's attention.

Saber must have heard it too because he frowned and spoke to Mika. "Tomasine isn't here. Give me your number and I'll get her to ring you."

"Not good enough." Mika's grip tightened and Emily groaned and attempted to twist free.

Gina appeared behind Mika, ghosting through the kitchen door. She held a gun in her hands, a look of determination on her face. The look of a warrior.

"Drop, Emily," Saber shouted.

She didn't hesitate, her weight falling without warning. A gun fired, the shot loud in the kitchen. Mika spun. A second shot echoed, and he toppled, the bloom of blood bright red against the cotton of his shirt.

"Come over here, Emily," Saber ordered. He wrapped his arms around his mate and held her, a wild expression on his face.

Gina stalked closer, a hard look on her chubby face, the gun still extended, ready to fire again.

Leo stooped to check the stranger's pulse. Mika didn't move. Not even when Gina crouched beside him. She checked his pulse too.

"Dead," she said.

"You okay?" Leo asked.

She nodded.

"I'll go and check on Isabella," Leo said.

Gina eyed him. "She's not there."

Acute disappointment flooded him since Gina's flat tone told him it was true. Even so, he had to see for himself. Leaving the kitchen, Leo hustled to his bedroom. Empty. The net curtain billowed in the breeze created by the open window.

"Damn." He thought they'd come to an understanding of sorts. Appeared not. Disillusioned and heartsick, he trudged to the kitchen. Right now his family needed him. He could try to sort out his personal life later.

"She gone?" Saber asked, looking up from Mika's body. Gina and Emily stood silently side by side.

"Must have left via the window."

Emily turned to glare at Gina. "What are you doing with a gun? You've shot a hole in my kitchen cupboard."

"She also saved you, sweetheart," Saber said. "One little hole isn't serious."

"But she has a gun," Emily repeated.

"Where did you get the gun?" Leo asked. "Did Isabella give it to you? Did she say anything when she went?" Okay, so he was officially sad. He couldn't stop thinking about his mate.

"The gun belongs to me," Gina said.

"What?" Emily shrieked. "Since when?"

"I have something to tell you," Gina said.

"You'd better not be pregnant," Saber snapped. "Tell me about the gun and what the hell you've been up to."

"I'm not pregnant," Gina said, her chubby body tensing at the charge.

Emily scowled. "Then why have you been sneaking around? You've given me gray hair."

"I...um..." The teenager sounded unusually diffident. "Oh shit," she said. "There's no easy way to do this." She stepped around the kitchen table until it stood between her and the three of them. A faint green glowed around her body.

Saber stiffened but Leo didn't take his eyes off Gina. The green grew brighter until it surrounded every inch of her chubby body.

"Damn, she's shifting," Saber said in astonishment.

"She's a leopard like the rest of you," Emily answered. "We've seen her shift before."

"Not with the green," Leo said, thinking back. "She always shifted in private where we couldn't see."

"I thought it was because she's shy," Emily said. "Not like the rest of you exhibitionists."

"She didn't take off her clothes this time," Saber said.

Leo could see Gina's body changing shape. She grew taller. Slimmer. The green died away leaving Isabella standing where Gina had stood seconds earlier. His mouth dropped open as he stared in shock. "*Isabella?*"

"Yeah. It's me," she said.

Horror filled Leo while he stared at her. He backed up until the cool stainless of the refrigerator halted his retreat. Gina. Isabella. They were the same person.

Saber frowned. "Which is the real one?"

Yeah, exactly the info he wanted. Not once had he blundered into wrong with Gina. She was a kid, for god's sake. Isabella, now... He shifted his weight, uncomfortable with the way his thoughts were veering.

"I am of age." Isabella straightened, her chin rising in defiance. "I am not a child."

"Fine," Leo said, his tone a big hint that he wasn't fine at all. "But what are you? You're not feline. Who are you?"

"Why the secrets?" Saber asked.

"I want to talk to Leo in private." Isabella stood at ease, her violet-blue eyes defiant while she made her demand.

"Wait. How do we know you won't harm him?" Saber asked. "What happened to the gun?"

"For goodness' sake," Isabella snapped. "If I'd wanted to hurt any of you, I could have done it ages ago." But she pulled a gun from her inside pocket plus a knife out of one of her boots and slapped them on the table. "The knife I keep in my other boot is the one I threw at Mika before Leo brought me back to the house. You can search me. I don't have any other weapons on me." She waited until it was obvious no one intended to take up her offer. Then, with a final glance at Leo, she stalked from the kitchen, her boots thudding on the wooden floor.

"What are you waiting for?" Emily demanded.

Leo exchanged a glance with Saber.

Saber shrugged. "The woman's right. She's lived with Tomasine and then us without hurting anyone. She killed him."

He indicated the dead mercenary with a jerk of his head. He reached for Emily's hand and squeezed it with obvious emotion. "Whoever she is, she's earned the right to have a private meeting with you."

Leo nodded, closed his eyes for an instant, trying to quell his panic. "I'm mated to her. I thought I knew her, but it turns out I don't."

Emily patted him on the shoulder. "Talk to her. I'm sure everything will turn out okay."

"What about him?" Leo asked. "We need to take care of him."

"I'll help Saber," Emily said. "I'm a Mitchell now. I can take the bad along with the good."

"And a fine Mitchell you are, sweetheart." Saber curled his arm around his wife's shoulders and pressed a kiss to her temple. "Let's take care of business and leave Leo to sort out things with his mate."

Leo nodded at Saber, gave Emily a quick kiss on the cheek and strode from the kitchen. Both nerves and concern combined to bounce around inside his stomach like a ping-pong ball on speed. Hell, he admitted it. He was out of his depth. He didn't know what to think. What did Isabella intend to tell him? With the lies and half-truths between them it was difficult to see a future.

Chapter 12

Truth

Isabella paced the length of Leo's bedroom, aware of the askew sensation, the sense of trespassing. Although she flirted with him in her Gina guise, she'd never pushed the bounds of propriety. She'd respected his privacy and tried not to dwell on the parade of woman through his life. Fear flared afresh. She loved the man, but had no idea how he'd react to the truth.

She could hear the soft murmur of voices in the kitchen. Leo, Saber and Emily. It wasn't difficult to guess the topic. Her. Was she trustworthy? What were they going to do with her? She huffed out an agitated breath and spun to make the return journey across the polished wooden floorboards. At least Felix and Tomasine could come out of hiding now. One positive in a host of negatives.

Mika had been the last of the mercenaries on the queen's trail. As long as Joseph died soon they'd be safe. No second chances for Joseph. Once she'd talked to Leo, she'd have a word with Saber and offer to do the job for free. It was the least she could do to repay the kindness Tomasine had shown her, saving her from a gang rape at the hand of the soldiers Joseph had sent to kill his brother, sister-in-law, niece.

Footsteps approached, and she froze. Leo appeared in the doorway. She took a deep breath and prayed she hadn't betrayed her agitation.

"Who are you?"

"Isabella Black." She wanted to add more but her throat knotted so tight it was difficult to force out the words. Swallowing didn't help.

Leo scowled and her heart fluttered. Even grumpy and surly looked good on the man. "What are you?"

"Shifter," she whispered hoarsely.

"You're something," Leo snapped. "We saw you transform."

His temper broke the communication barrier, unblocked her throat. "Do you think this is easy? Do you think I liked the lies, the subterfuge?"

"The lies can't have bothered you too much," Leo fired back. "You used me, used my family."

"No!"

"Yes," he mocked, stepping into the room and closing the door behind him. "What sort of shifter?"

She swallowed hard, lifted her chin and boldly met his gaze. "Chameleon." She'd done the best she could in the circumstances. Damn if she intended to apologize. She glanced at him, saw the drift of his gaze toward her heaving breasts.

Maybe, she'd just throw herself at him again, finish the mating bond and go through the rest of their lives proving her love, her good character. Isabella took half a step toward him before she realized she couldn't use smoke screens any longer. From now on she needed to tell the truth, no matter how much it hurt her chances with Leo. Isabella turned away and walked over to Leo's bed, sinking onto it with a soft sigh of reluctance. Leo deserved the truth. "I'm a chameleon shifter."

"Which means what?"

"It means I can take on any shape I desire. I don't have to remove my clothes and objects such as weapons morph with me if I'm wearing them on my person at the time."

"Why haven't I heard of chameleons before?"

"Full of questions, aren't you?" she mocked.

"I want the truth." He met her gaze and held it.

Isabella looked away first, her heart thudding erratically. No doubt he could hear her turmoil. "What else do you want to know?"

"Why me?"

A laugh escaped. "Leo, have you looked in the mirror lately? You're gorgeous. The women look at you and start wanting."

Leo stiffened, his expression going impassive. "I'm more than a pretty face." Distaste shaded his tone.

"You are. You're kind, intelligent, good at your job at the vineyard. You're always ready to help out on the farm. You're sexy, good in bed. And that's just a start. Why wouldn't I want you?"

A glow lit his green eyes. "Is this your real form?" He gestured at her body, his attention sending a surge of nervousness swirling through her stomach.

"It's my real human form." Please don't let him ask. *Please*. She was so...ugly.

"And your nonhuman form?"

"Not important. Do you have any more questions?"

His eyes narrowed. "Yeah, just one before we move on to other things. Are we safe? Are there more mercenaries out there?"

"That's two questions."

"Cut the cute act, Isabella. I want to know if my family is safe."

"The mercenaries Joseph contracted are dead apart from me. Once Joseph is gone I think that should be the end of it."

Leo nodded but continued to frown. "Are you sure they're dead?"

"I killed them." Which didn't show her in a good light. She opened her mouth to defend herself and halted. It was her job. She would not apologize.

"Okay." Leo strolled over to the bed and sat, close but still not touching. "So if the mercenaries are dead, what are you going to do now?"

Instantly her throat tightened again. What she wanted and what she ended up with were two different things. She edged away. She couldn't think with him sitting so close. Her nipples prickled while her pussy moistened. All she needed to do was lean a fraction to the right and they'd touch. "No idea."

His expression froze, as if he knew she lied. Then he lifted his hand to cup her cheek. Her heart skipped a beat, and she stared in consternation, too startled to do anything sensible such as seducing him. "I'd believe you if I couldn't smell your desire."

"Leo," she whispered, the sound full of longing. Isabella wanted to ask him what this meant because she was confused.

"We can discuss the rest later, Isabella, but right now I need to fuck you. Make love," he added in a husky voice. "You scared me half to death. I want...need to..." he trailed off with a helpless shrug, but Isabella understood his need to reaffirm life because she felt it too.

She buried her face in his chest and clutched his shoulders, breathing in his special scent, listening to his breathing, the clang of pots and the murmur of voices at the other end of the house. Leo's hands glided over her back, pressing her against him so every muscle and his partially erect cock brushed her body. The site of her bullet wound throbbed, tender but healed now thanks to her shifter genes. She never considered moving away to ease the ache because this was where she needed to be—in Leo's arms.

He nuzzled the soft skin of her neck and slipped his tongue beneath the collar of her shirt to rasp across her mark. A moan whispered from her at the surge of heat, the promise of pleasure in his touch.

"More," she demanded.

"You know what this is?" He paused, waiting for her answer.

"Tomasine told me about feline marks."

"Good." A wealth of satisfaction throbbed in his reply, but Isabella worried. Yes, she loved him, his family, and they didn't seem too concerned about her occupation. She was still in the Mitchell homestead and with Leo. They hadn't kicked her out. Yet.

"Enough for now." He tipped back her head and stared into her eyes, his lips curving into a gentle smile. "Betcha, I can get naked quicker than you."

He laughed and ripped off his clothes before Isabella had a chance to blink. Boots and socks first. His shirt dropped to the floor, his jeans kicked aside, and he pushed his boxers down his muscled thighs, baring his muscular body. Isabella had removed her shirt.

"Told ya I'd win."

"I was distracted," Isabella said, scrambling out of her jeans.

"Stop. I'll do the rest." Leo swung her into his arms and dropped her on the bed. He smoothed his hand over one lace-clad breast, the exquisite friction bringing a sigh of surrender. She was his. No arguments there at all.

She yanked him closer, mouth blindly searching for his. It wasn't a gentle kiss. Teeth clashed before they achieved the perfect fit. Isabella bit his lips, tormenting him before soothing the nip with her tongue.

Breathing hard, he pulled away, his eyes caressing each part of her. With purposeful moves, he stripped off her bra and panties before kissing the hollow at her throat. He licked the valley between her breasts then squeezed them together, sucking on one nipple while his fingers teased the other. Sweet, agonizing circles of his tongue, nips with his teeth and gentle tugs until her nipples tingled and her breathing became harsh, her body highly sensitized and an empty ache in her pussy.

Isabella slipped her hand between their bodies to grip his silken shaft, her thumb brushing across the tip. She smoothed the beads of pre-cum away from his slit, loving the idea she could make him feel desire. Leo made a dark sound and wrestled control from her and caged her with his arms.

"You want me. I can smell your arousal."

Isabella grinned. "Nothing gets past you."

"Damn right." He kissed a path across her rib cage and over her hipbone.

She drew in an unsteady breath, her body tingling from his administrations. Each touch, each stroke of fingers. His tongue rasped along her cleft, pushing a jolt of sharp sensation through her. Each time with Leo was special. His hands and mouth searched for pleasure points, touches both light and teasing. She gasped, arching up into him, her head shifting from side to side.

"Leo." His name a fervent prayer of need.

Thankfully, he moved over her, handling her with urgency, but each stroke of his fingers spoke of more than lust. It spoke of love. Her eyes misted at the thought. Did she belong after all? Could they have a future despite the secrets still standing between them? His cock pushed into her, and she was his.

His hard body covered hers, and he stroked hard while his lips slid over her mark. The sensations raced across her pleasure points, consumed her until she shattered, flying into a series of fiery explosions. She held him tight, drawing his scent deep, so she'd always remember making love with him.

Leo thrust twice and stilled, his breath whooshing out in a long sigh of pleasure. He separated their bodies and drew her back into his arms.

"I love you, Isabella." Leo caressed her naked back.

Both the words and his touch intensified the sense of belonging. Isabella knew she could get by without saying another word but honesty propelled her onward. She couldn't live with lies, needed nothing but truth between them.

"I...I love you too. I have for a long time," she added with a rush. "Since the first time I saw you."

"That long, huh?" Leo smoothed his hand over her hair, the warmth of his palm soaking into her scalp.

"Yeah." Isabella made a sleepy sound and cuddled closer, prevaricating for a few seconds. She understood what she needed to do. Pulling from Leo's grasp, she stood on tottery legs. With two unsteady steps, she stepped away from the bed.

"What is it?" A sexy smile played around his mouth as he propped his body up, weight placed on his left arm.

"I'm working up the courage to show you my true natural form."

"It can't be that bad, sweetheart."

Isabella considered the color green. Not her favorite. She glanced at Leo and saw reassurance in his green eyes. Okay, there were exceptions. Her breasts moved when she inhaled, then with a sigh, she pictured the creature—her natural form.

The normal soft green glow shone around her form like a halo. Bones reshaped, the pull on her face feeling worse than usual because her mind fought the change. Easy to tell why. Both head and heart worried about Leo's reaction. A groan squeezed past her lips and she sank to the floor, short, stubby limbs no longer able to hold her upright. The green glow dissipated and she watched Leo bolt upright. Her huge, round eyes blinked and inside she cried.

Ugly. *So ugly.*

Bright green scales covered her low-slung body and her tail swung from side to side in agitation.

"Isabella."

The shock on his face was expected but at least he hadn't run from the room. She stared at him unblinkingly, sick at heart. Gregory, a former lover had laughed in her face, telling her he'd never commit to someone as ugly as her. She'd tried to tell him, she could take any form and hardly ever looked this way, but it hadn't mattered to him. He'd seen her in her true form and couldn't get past the truth.

She looked like a lizard—an ugly, spike-covered green lizard. Not an appropriate mate for a sleek and strong tiger shifter

Gregory had said. Her mouth moved, sharp white teeth clacking together.

"Isabella," Leo said. "You're cute."

Cute? She blinked, white lids screening her sight until she regained control. *Cute?*

Leo stood, his eyes resting on her scaly form. "Can I come closer? Touch you?"

A sharp croak emerged, and she swished her tail. He wanted to touch her? Her heart thudded, surprise and shock filling her. No one had touched her since she was a child, not in this form. Yearning crawled through her. The gift of touch. When she left she'd remember this moment, remember Leo with fondness until her dying day.

"I guess that means yes," Leo said in lazy humor.

Isabella croaked again in distress. She backed up until the tip of her tail hit a wooden dressing table.

"Come on, don't be a baby. You can touch me. Just let me have my turn first."

Confused, she blinked and croaked for a third time. It was the one reaction she could manage. She thought she knew Leo, but instead of showing disgust, he displayed curiosity, actually wanting to touch her ugly body.

"Such a pretty color." Leo crouched beside her, moving without haste as if he understood her spooked thoughts. "I think green will be my favorite color from now on." He ran the tips of his fingers across her cheek and she felt the delicate touch to the tip of her tail. "Yeah, such a gorgeous shade and so cute with those big eyes. Saber and Emily will love you, just as I do."

He loved her? Still?

His husky voice soothed her, lulling her into a calmer state while his fingers grew daring, caressing her spine. He rubbed around a sharp spine and across her head. Isabella watched his expression the entire time, trying to judge his reaction, watch for distaste. It didn't happen. Instead, he looked entranced. Curious.

"Saber! Emily!" he called without warning.

Isabella let out a distressed cry, so loud it echoed in the bedroom. Footsteps thundered along the hall and the bedroom door crashed open. Isabella croaked twice.

"Don't shift," Leo said. "Please." He glanced at Saber and Emily. "Isn't Isabella cute?"

"Ooh, what a beautiful green," Emily said.

"Natural form?" Saber asked.

"Yeah." Leo stroked across her head and she trembled.

"Interesting," Emily said, glancing at Leo. A smile played across her lips as she looked him up and down. "Your natural form is very nice too. Of course not as sexy as Saber—"

Saber slapped his hand across her eyes and growled at the back of his throat. "Put on some clothes. I dislike my mate ogling other men, and not my brother. Cover yourself."

Leo chuckled, grabbed his jeans and stepped into them.

Isabella decided she'd had enough of show and tell. She pictured another form in her mind and shifted, the green glow lighting the room. "I'll leave now," she said.

"Sweetheart...hell, did you have to do that?"

Emily clawed Saber's hand from her eyes, looked at Isabella and giggled. "Two Leos. Just what we need."

"Isabella, it's disconcerting seeing my face staring at me. Could you please change to Isabella?"

Isabella shifted again but retained a male form. She strolled up to Leo and kissed him on the lips, letting her stubbled cheek brush his. Her body reacted in a masculine manner.

Emily giggled again and even Saber smirked.

"Isabella!" Leo rolled his eyes, but she noticed they twinkled.

The peal of the phone interrupted and Saber prowled off to answer.

"Maybe I'll leave you to it," Emily said, her wry glance darting over the pair.

"Don't you care that I'm ugly in my natural form?" Isabella asked.

Emily shook her head. "You might not look like everyone's idea of beauty, Isabella, but you're such a pretty color."

"It's what inside that matters," Leo added.

"But you don't know me very well."

"Rubbish," Emily said. "You're loyal, determined, loving. You're part of the family."

"You're my mate, Isabella." Leo trailed his hand over her cheek, getting over his discomfort at cuddling a male, since it was Isabella's eyes that gazed at him.

"It's done. Joseph is dead," Saber said, entering the bedroom again. "Our contact has confirmed the kill."

"It's over?" Emily asked.

"It is if Joseph is gone," Isabella said. "I can double-check with my sources, if you want."

Saber nodded. "Excellent. Come on, Emily. Let's leave these two alone. I want to ring Felix." He ushered Emily out and shut the bedroom door behind them, leaving Isabella with Leo.

"You don't mind my appearance?" She couldn't believe he didn't care, not after she'd had her ugliness drummed into her since childhood.

Leo cupped her masculine face and stared into her eyes. He smiled and kissed her slow and easy. He grasped her hips and pulled her tight against his body. The sensation electrified her, two cocks brushing together. She moaned, entranced by the feel of his lips and the emotions coursing through mind and body. When they pulled apart, they were both breathing hard.

"I've never considered making love with a male before, not until you. I love you, Isabella." He stood back to admire her naked form. "On the bed."

He shucked his jeans without taking his eyes off her and joined her, their masculine bodies rubbing together.

"Sweetheart, I'll love you no matter what form you're in. I'm even willing to get kinky and experiment." His eyes glowed, and he glanced at her straining cock before meeting her gaze again. "But for this I want the Isabella I've come to know." He smiled at her, putting a wealth of emotion into motion between them. "I want you to prove you love me."

"There's one more thing I have to tell you, Leo." She pictured her Isabella form and morphed into a feminine shape, her naked body brushing Leo's.

"No matter what we'll work it out."

"How can you tell it's something bad?"

"The cute little pucker of concentration between your brows."

Isabella inhaled sharply to prepare herself. It didn't work, so she blurted out the truth. "I can't have children, Leo. Not with you."

His smile died and her stomach hollowed in alarm. She'd known things were too good to be true. After everything she'd done, she didn't deserve a happy ending.

"I'd like children one day."

It felt as if he'd kicked her in the gut. Pain, sharp and jagged ripped through her. She blinked, a tight knot in her throat. "It won't be with me. I'll leave." Isabella attempted dignity, squeezing the words out, desperate not to cry.

"Can you have children with someone else?"

She struggled to rise but Leo refused to release her.

"Isabella?"

"With another chameleon. Doubtful since there's few of us left."

He nodded. "It doesn't matter. Maybe we can adopt, if that's what you want. We'll work something out. Isabella, you're my mate. You're not putting me off. It's time to show me you love me." Truth rang in his voice and she believed what he said, that he wanted her and they'd work something out together.

He... Isabella gasped, a crazy mixture of hope and fear catapulting around in the pit of her stomach. She loved him, had wanted him since the first moment he'd walked into Tomasine's rented house. That want had transformed to love.

Her mind cleared and her thoughts narrowed in on what to do. Simple. She relaxed against his muscular body, fitting her curves to his chest. Isabella smiled up at him. Pressed a kiss to his jaw, another to his mouth. He ran his hand across her shoulder, his touch firm and persuasive, inviting her to continue. She sighed with pleasure, her body tingling from the contact. After placing a quick trail of kisses down his neck, her tongue flicked out to lick his collarbone. He quivered at the contact.

"More," he gasped, baring his neck to her.

Her teeth grazed the fleshy part of his neck, teasing him before she clamped them tight. The coppery taste of his life force filled her mouth as she completed the feline mating. She licked across the wound, her saliva working in the same manner as a feline shifter. He moaned, breathing hard and trembling.

Smiling, she gripped his shoulders and lifted her head, letting every bit of her love for him show. "I love you, Leo."

His sharp inhalation filled her with satisfaction. One moment they were chest to chest, the next she lay facedown on the bed. Leo grasped her hips and lifted her to a kneeling position, his fingers stroking her swollen folds. She felt the prod of his erection and gasped at the seamless thrust that left him fully embedded in her pussy. His cock throbbed, leaving her full but still needy.

"Isabella," he said, his tone of awe bringing a shiver of pleasure.

He set up a hard and fast rhythm, curving his body over hers and nibbling at her mark. Her vagina clasped his cock hard the instant his teeth scraped over her flesh. Leo thrust steadily while sliding one finger across her swollen clit. One touch was all it took, and she shattered. Leo's cock pulsed, his big body trembling with the force of his release. A lazy lick over her mark set off a series of small aftershocks.

"I love you, Leo," she murmured.

Leo separated their bodies before dragging her back into his arms. "Good because my heart is yours, sweetheart."

"What am I going to do now?"

"Retire? We can find you something else to occupy your time."

"I intended to retire," she said. "I don't want to kill again, not unless someone attacks me first."

"There's no hurry." Leo kissed her, taking his time. When they pulled apart, they were both breathing heavily. "A honeymoon first. I want time alone with you," he added with a wink. "I'm thinking kinky."

"Sounds good." Isabella smiled. Excellent. Waking up in Leo's arms and knowing they belonged together. It was the stuff of dreams. Her dreams. She sighed—a hum of happy satisfaction. She had a home. "Together," she murmured, stroking his face. "Always together."

"You betcha, sweetheart," he said. "Together." And then he kissed her, this kiss different, better because now she had a real future ahead of her, a future with the man she loved.

Epilogue

One month later, Mitchell residence, Middlemarch

L eo grabbed Isabella's hand as she paced along the gravel path winding between Emily's flowerbeds. "Stop pacing. It will be fine. You've spoken to Tomasine via phone and confessed everything. She wasn't angry."

Isabella squeezed his fingers before pulling free. She didn't cease her restless strides. She'd grown used to facing Tomasine and Sylvie in her Gina guise. Despite the cute sundress and her immaculate blonde hair, she felt naked now. Off-balance.

How could Tom forgive her after what she'd done?

Isabella stopped near a bed of yellow daises. Twitchy fingers plucked a bloom and tossed it aside. She'd concealed the truth the entire time they'd been together. Tomasine had saved her life, stopped what would have been rape...

Tom had saved her and she'd...lied.

"Isabella." Her mate approached her, humor shining in his expression. "You'd better stop denuding Emily's plants before she calls a team of assassins on you."

"What?" Isabella blinked and saw she'd picked at least ten flowers. They carpeted the ground at her feet, splashes of sunshine-yellow against the gravel footpath. "Crap."

"Where is she?" a feminine voice called.

Someone—Isabella thought it was Emily—answered and the thud of rushing feet beat in time with her anxious heart. Tomasine burst from the double doors of the lounge and onto the deck, glanced around the garden and spotted them. For an instant, the petite woman froze, then she sprinted toward them.

A gurgle of panic escaped Isabella, and Leo stepped to her side, the gentle weight of his hand on her shoulder the only thing keeping her from bolting.

Felix stepped into the garden with Sylvie at his side. He was a slightly older version of Leo, except his features were harsher, giving him a stern look. Five-year-old Sylvie had grown taller while they'd been away. Dressed in shorts and a pink T-shirt, with her black hair loose, she was just as scary as Tomasine. They approached and panic bubbled inside Isabella. Every muscle in her body tensed, the urge to flee kicking her with spikes of adrenaline.

"Easy, sweetheart," Leo murmured.

Tomasine pulled up a few feet from them and cocked her head, her black hair gleaming in the sun. She'd lost the ever-present tension and now bore a few freckles on her nose. "Gina, is that really you?"

"Y-yes." Isabella cleared her throat and tried again. "Yes, it's me."

"Where is Gina?" Sylvie demanded, her gaze passing over Isabella in dismissal.

"Sylvie," Felix said. "Remember, we explained that Gina would be different once we came home."

"I won't see Gina ever again?" A tear streaked down Sylvie's face.

"It's Isabella," Leo said.

"You helped us stay alive all this time," Tomasine said.

Isabella edged closer to Leo, overwhelmed by the attention. The shadows beneath the trees beckoned—a place to hide.

"Thank you," Tomasine said, and she threw herself at Isabella, her petite built belying her strength.

Isabella took half a pace back before she regained her equilibrium. Leo stepped aside to greet his brother, and their quiet murmurs helped Isabella to quell her inner panic.

Tomasine released her grip and placed an arm's width of distance between them. "Thank you, Isabella. I couldn't understand how we managed to keep ahead of the team of assassins. In the end, I told myself it was good luck, that we were due some, but all the time we had our own personal guardian angel. Why didn't you tell me?"

"I-I..." Isabella trailed off, more nonplussed than she'd ever felt before.

Thankfully, Leo stepped in to help. "Isabella wasn't sure you'd trust her, Tomasine. Working undercover gave her a better way of helping to keep you safe."

Tomasine frowned and slowly nodded. "I wouldn't have trusted you. You're right. But a teenage girl...I couldn't help but try to shelter you from the worst."

"I want Gina," Sylvie said, pouting. "I want to tell her about the farm."

"Show her," Leo said. "Shift to Gina for her then transform back to Isabella. It will help her understand."

Isabella glanced at Tomasine. "Is that all right?"

"Of course it is. I have to admit to curiosity myself. I know you're speaking the truth, but my mind is fighting it," Tomasine said.

Isabella stepped back to give herself more space. She centered her mind and shifted to chubby teenager Gina.

"Incredible," Felix said.

"I'm jealous," Tomasine said. "You didn't have to remove any clothes to shift."

"Gina!" Sylvie shouted and threw herself at Isabella. Her skinny arms clung. "We had so much fun at the farm. I shifted to a kitty and we ran lots."

"You still chatter a lot," Isabella said in Gina's voice.

"Let Gina go, so she can shift back," Felix said.

"Sylvie," Tomasine chided when her daughter didn't move.

Sylvie reluctantly released her and Isabella retreated. Perhaps she'd shift to a slightly different form to help Sylvie. She

207

morphed into the same clothes she'd worn the night she'd discovered Sylvie in feline form.

Sylvie gaped. "You helped me," she whispered. "When I turned into a kitty."

"I did," Isabella said. "I could see you needed a little help."

Emily appeared on the deck. "I've made a cup of tea. I have sandwiches and kitty cupcakes."

"Yay!" Sylvie clapped her hands together.

"Wait." Isabella morphed to an identical version of Sylvie.

"That's me," Sylvie said.

"I'm really Isabella." Isabella changed back to her Isabella form, surprising a giggle from Sylvie. "Should we go and get a cupcake before Saber and Emily eat them all?" She held out her hand and her heart twisted when Sylvie placed her small hand in hers.

"That's incredible," Tomasine said.

"Could have interesting applications," Felix said.

Tomasine elbowed him in the ribs. "Behave."

"My mate is incredible," Leo agreed, pride filling his words. Love.

Isabella winked at him before she and Sylvie entered the house.

"Good timing," Emily said. "Saber has just popped open the sparkling wine."

"We're celebrating?" Leo asked when they all surrounded the kitchen table.

Emily had kitten cupcakes, sandwiches, stacks of cups and saucers and glasses of wine waiting for them.

"We are," Emily confirmed. "I now have two sisters-in-law to help me keep the Mitchell brothers in line." She handed out glasses of wine and a small one with a different-colored beverage for Sylvie.

"Hey," Felix said. "We're well-behaved."

"Sometimes." Tomasine glanced at Saber. "Can I make the toast?"

Saber nodded.

She lifted her glass. "To Isabella who has helped us become the family we are today. To family."

"To family!" everyone chorused.

"To my mate," Leo whispered. His body heat seared her bare arm, his closeness bringing a spike to her pulse rate. "The love of my life."

Saber overheard and grinned. "To love and our beautiful mates."

Isabella glanced at the circle of faces—her family now—and smiled so wide her facial muscles ached. Her gaze met with Tomasine's and all she saw was approval and...and love. The residual panic in her faded. "Thank you for bringing me into your family. You saved me as much as I saved you."

"That's what family do," Tomasine said.

The wine tickled Isabella's nose as she took another sip. Leo slipped his arm around her waist and she leaned into him, fully secure in his love. The future had never seemed so inviting.

Bonus Chapter

Mitchell Farm, Middlemarch, New Zealand

Feline Shapeshifter Council Meeting.

Present: Saber Mitchell, Sid Blackburn, Kenneth Nesbitt, Agnes Paisley, Valerie McClintock, Benjamin Urquart

Saber Mitchell cocked his head, and seconds later, the doorbell chimed. He checked his watch. Early. Damn, he was never going to finish his bookwork for the accountants at this rate.

He pushed away from his desk and stomped to answer the door. "Yes."

Kenneth Nesbitt, big and hefty, nodded a greeting. He plucked a handkerchief from his shorts pocket and scrubbed it over his sweaty face. "Damn hot today."

"Yes." Saber turned to Sid Blackburn for clarification. His scalp gleamed through his thin white hair.

The peacemaker of their group, his wrinkled face bore distinct worry. "We have a situation, lad. Needs an urgent discussion. Ah, here are the others now."

Saber stood aside and ushered Kenneth and Sid inside. He waited for Agnes, Valerie and Benjamin to make their way up the footpath to the door.

Five minutes later, they all sat around the kitchen table, cups of tea and coffee to hand. Kenneth munched on a chocolate chip cookie.

"Now tell me why you're here an hour early," Saber said.

Benjamin tapped his fingers on the tabletop. "Let's get the other stuff out of the way first."

"But you've come early. It must be—" Saber broke off. He should know better than to try to direct their meetings. "All right. How are things going with the zombie run? Emily and I have done some more research and mapped out a possible course. Five kilometers in length is the usual. Not all of the races have obstacles, but we thought a mud run, a rope climb and perhaps a water crossing would add fun. Maybe six obstacles in all. It should be easy enough to think of a few more to challenge the runners."

Agnes picked up a pink cookie, studied it and took a cautious bite. Saber grinned since Felix's daughter Sylvie had helped Emily make cookies for their meeting. It must've passed the taste test because she took another bite and drank some of her tea.

Valerie McClintock peered through her smudged glasses lenses. "Anyone will be able to enter the race, but what about our shifters competing against the humans? They will have an advantage."

"Emily thought of that," Saber said. "There will be individual and team prizes. All teams will consist of four people and there must be at least two humans in each team."

"Hmm," Agnes said. "We should have mixed teams. I think that was mentioned at the last meeting? Make that a rule too. After all, the purpose is to get the young men and women together."

Sid nodded. "I like that idea." He picked up his pen and jotted notes on one of the pads Emily had left for them. "How much are we charging for an entry fee? And how much are we giving back for prizes?"

"I'll work that out," Valerie said. "Saber, give me your estimates to set up the course and any other associated costs, and I'll take it from there. Did the local businesses come up with ideas?"

"Yes, we have several ideas that might work," Kenneth said, mopping at his face yet again. "I'll present them at the next meeting since there are still a few coming in."

"Good. Good." Benjamin nodded. "We're all agreed, and we'll finalize details at the next meeting."

Saber frowned and scanned their faces. None of the council members seemed themselves today. "What else is going on?" he demanded.

Benjamin sighed. "It's Marsh and Caroline Rutherford."

"The Rutherfords—the property at the far end of the valley?" Saber asked. "Dawn and Charles? Their son?"

"Yes, the Rutherfords are family friends," Agnes said, her voice querulous and unforgiving. "Marsh and Caroline live on the farm. Dawn told me they're planning to separate."

Valerie tsked. "They have two young boys. One is six and the other is four. Dawn said Caroline intends to take her children to the city."

Saber reined in his confusion and tried to follow the conversation.

"The fool boy has never told his wife he's a feline. His parents have never approved of his marriage to a human," Kenneth said. "He's never marked her. She has no idea her sons will shift once they become teenagers."

"He never marked her?" Saber asked in disbelief. He recalled how it had been with him and Emily. The idea of not marking her...

Ben's coffee mug thumped on the tabletop. "His parents told him it was for the best, and Caroline doesn't understand all the sneaking around. Of course, the boy wants to shift and run. It's our nature. His young wife doesn't understand his absences." He speared a glance at Agnes. "Charles isn't an easy man. Rumor says he's dangled the farm like a carrot in front of Marsh. It's obvious the boy loves the land, but Charles doesn't let him have any autonomy. My guess is that financially, Marsh can't afford to leave the farm. I doubt Charles pays him a fair wage."

"That's not good news, but what does it have to do with me?" Saber asked.

"You'll speak with them," Agnes said, reaching for another pink cookie. "You and Emily can talk to them together. Bang their heads together if necessary. Those young boys will need guidance. I knew it was a mistake for Marsh and Caroline to live near his parents."

"I'm not interfering in the man's marriage," Saber said.

"But you're mated to a human. You can help them understand or at least see the consequences of what might happen if the boys don't learn of their heritage," Kenneth said.

No. Hell, no, he refused to become involved or to drag Emily into the middle of this mess. "What about Marsh's parents?"

Agnes snorted. "This is partly their fault. If they hadn't interfered or allowed their prejudices to interfere in their son's marriage, we wouldn't have this mess. Think of those two small boys, Saber."

This had the makings of a disaster. An embarrassing one. "Why does it have to be me?"

"Because you're a similar age, and because Emily has a good head on her shoulders. Together you might be able to make Caroline see reason."

"What about Marsh?" Saber asked tartly. "Shouldn't he tell his parents to butt out of his marriage?"

"Sid or Benjamin will take care of that part," Valerie said. "We figured that would work best. Dawn and Charles might listen to Sid or Benjamin."

"Let me think about it," Saber said.

"Discuss it with Emily." Agnes took another bite of her cookie.

"We're going to speak with Dawn and Charles Rutherford this evening," Sid said. "We'll send Marsh and Caroline to see you. Perhaps you could invite them to dinner, make it more relaxing for you all."

Fuck. "Felix and Leo are coming for dinner tonight and bringing their mates. It's Sylvie's birthday."

"Excellent," Benjamin said. "We'll send the boys along too."

"But-but I—"

"You're a good lad," Valerie said and leaned closer to pat his hand. "You'll do the right thing for Middlemarch and those two small boys."

Saber's shoulders slumped as he felt the sting of defeat. He knew when he was beaten.

Agnes popped to her feet. "We'll be off then." She snagged the last pink cookie and took a huge bite.

Sid stood too, his demeanor serious. "Should we tell them six o'clock for dinner?"

"Fine," Saber snapped, and that seemed to be the signal for everyone to depart. They scuttled from his house like rats deserting a sinking ship, except their faces bore satisfaction at a job well done.

Saber closed the door behind them, sighed and picked up the phone. He was *really* looking forward to telling Emily about this newest assignment.

Thank you for reading MY ASSASSIN.

Have the Feline Council set Saber an impossible task when they asked him to speak with Caroline and Marsh about their marriage? Saber doesn't want to poke his nose in where it's not wanted, yet those young boys won't thrive in the city with their human mother, who knows nothing of shifters.

Read Caroline and Marsh's story in

MY ESTRANGED LOVER.
(www.shelleymunro.com/books/my-estranged-lover/)

"Another great story in the Middlemarch Shifters series, this one brings a whole new perspective and introduces new characters and scenery for readers to enjoy. The cute and precocious child in this story added quite a few surprises and a few chuckles to my delight...I can't wait for my next visit." ~Stormy Vixen Book Reviews

About Author

USA Today bestselling author Shelley Munro lives in Auckland, the City of Sails, with her husband and a cheeky Jack Russell/mystery breed dog.

Typical New Zealanders, Shelley and her husband left home for their big OE soon after they married (translation of New Zealand speak - big overseas experience). A twelve-month-long adventure lengthened to six years of roaming the world. Enduring memories include being almost sat on by a mountain gorilla in Rwanda, lazing on white sandy beaches in India, whale watching in Alaska, searching for leprechauns in Ireland, and dealing with ghosts in an English pub.

While travel is still a big attraction, these days Shelley is most likely found in front of her computer following another love - that of writing stories of contemporary and paranormal romance and adventure. Other interests include watching

SHELLEY MUNRO

rugby (strictly for research purposes), cycling, playing croquet and the ukelele, and curling up with an enjoyable book.

Visit Shelley at her Website
www.shelleymunro.com

Join Shelley's Newsletter www.shelleymunro.com/newsletter

Visit Shelley's Facebook page
www.facebook.com/ShelleyMunroAuthor

Follow Shelley at Bookbub
www.bookbub.com/authors/shelley-munro

Also By Shelley

Paranormal

Middlemarch Shifters
My Scarlet Woman
My Younger Lover
My Peeping Tom
My Assassin
My Estranged Lover
My Feline Protector
My Determined Suitor
My Cat Burglar
My Stray Cat
My Second Chance
My Plan B
My Cat Nap
My Romantic Tangle
My Blue Lady
My Twin Trouble
My Precious Gift

Middlemarch Gathering

My Highland Mate

My Highland Fling

Middlemarch Capture

Snared by Saber

Favored by Felix

Lost with Leo

Spellbound with Sly

Journey with Joe

Star-Crossed with Scarlett

Lightning Source UK Ltd.
Milton Keynes UK
UKHW010711251122
412773UK00002B/289